THE QUEEN WAS DEFINITELY NOT AMUSED.

Murder and royalty didn't mix. Princess Helena had only a distant claim to the throne, but when her friends and lovers began turning up dead, Buckingham Palace demanded to know the reason why.

The princess, it appeared, had a wildly wicked streak. It might have been elegant entertainment indeed, squiring Her reckless young Royal Highness through her dutiful official days and licentious London nights. But Supt. Perry Trethowan, Scotland Yard, had precious little time for pleasure if he meant to stop a cold-blooded killer intent on blue-blooded murder and prevent the scandal that would shake the nation.

SCENE OF THE CRIME® MYSTERIES

2 A MEDIUM FOR MURDER, *Mignon Warner*
4 DEATH OF A MYSTERY WRITER, *Robert Barnard*
6 DEATH AFTER BREAKFAST, *Hugh Pentecost*
8 THE POISONED CHOCOLATES CASE, *Anthony Berkeley*
10 A SPRIG OF SEA LAVENDER, *J. R. L. Anderson*
12 WATSON'S CHOICE, *Gladys Mitchell*
14 SPENCE AND THE HOLIDAY MURDERS, *Michael Allen*
16 THE TAROT MURDERS, *Mignon Warner*
18 DEATH ON THE HIGH C's, *Robert Barnard*
20 WINKING AT THE BRIM, *Gladys Mitchell*
22 TRIAL AND ERROR, *Anthony Berkeley*
24 RANDOM KILLER, *Hugh Pentecost*
26 SPENCE AT THE BLUE BAZAAR, *Michael Allen*
28 GENTLY WITH THE INNOCENTS, *Alan Hunter*
30 THE JUDAS PAIR, *Jonathan Gash*
32 DEATH OF A LITERARY WIDOW, *Robert Barnard*
34 THE TWELVE DEATHS OF CHRISTMAS, *Marian Babson*
36 GOLD BY GEMINI, *Jonathan Gash*
38 LANDED GENTLY, *Alan Hunter*
40 MURDER, MURDER LITTLE STAR, *Marian Babson*
42 DEATH IN A COLD CLIMATE, *Robert Barnard*
44 A CHILD'S GARDEN OF DEATH, *Richard Forrest*
46 GENTLY THROUGH THE WOODS, *Alan Hunter*
48 THE GRAIL TREE, *Jonathan Gash*
50 RULING PASSION, *Reginald Hill*
52 DEATH OF A PERFECT MOTHER, *Robert Barnard*
54 A COFFIN FROM THE PAST, *Gwendoline Butler*
56 AND ONE FOR THE DEAD, *Pierre Audemars*
58 DEATH ON THE HEATH, *Alan Hunter*
60 DEATH BY SHEER TORTURE, *Robert Barnard*
62 SLAY ME A SINNER, *Pierre Audemars*
64 DEATH IN TIME, *Mignon Warner*
66 DEATH AND THE PRINCESS, *Robert Barnard*

MURDER INK.® MYSTERIES

1 DEATH IN THE MORNING, *Sheila Radley*
3 THE BRANDENBURG HOTEL, *Pauline Glen Winslow*
5 McGARR AND THE SIENESE CONSPIRACY, *Bartholomew Gill*
7 THE RED HOUSE MYSTERY, *A. A. Milne*
9 THE MINUTEMAN MURDERS, *Jane Langton*
11 MY FOE OUTSTRETCH'D BENEATH THE TREE, *V. C. Clinton-Baddeley*
13 GUILT EDGED, *W. J. Burley*
15 COPPER GOLD, *Pauline Glen Winslow*
17 MANY DEADLY RETURNS, *Patricia Moyes*
19 McGARR AT THE DUBLIN HORSE SHOW, *Bartholomew Gill*
21 DEATH AND LETTERS, *Elizabeth Daly*
23 ONLY A MATTER OF TIME, *V. C. Clinton-Baddeley*
25 WYCLIFFE AND THE PEA-GREEN BOAT, *W. J. Burley*
27 ANY SHAPE OR FORM, *Elizabeth Daly*
29 COFFIN SCARCELY USED, *Colin Watson*
31 THE CHIEF INSPECTOR'S DAUGHTER, *Sheila Radley*
33 PREMEDICATED MURDER, *Douglas Clark*
35 NO CASE FOR THE POLICE, *V. C. Clinton-Baddeley*
37 JUST WHAT THE DOCTOR ORDERED, *Colin Watson*
39 DANGEROUS DAVIES, *Leslie Thomas*
41 THE GIMMEL FLASK, *Douglas Clark*
43 SERVICE OF ALL THE DEAD, *Colin Dexter*
45 DEATH'S BRIGHT DART, *V. C. Clinton-Baddeley*
47 GOLDEN RAIN, *Douglas Clark*
49 THE MAN WITH A LOAD OF MISCHIEF, *Martha Grimes*
51 DOWN AMONG THE DEAD MEN, *Patricia Moyes*
53 HOPJOY WAS HERE, *Colin Watson*
55 NIGHTWALK, *Elizabeth Daly*
57 SITUATION TRAGEDY, *Simon Brett*
59 CHARITY ENDS AT HOME, *Colin Watson*
61 JOHNNY UNDER GROUND, *Patricia Moyes*
63 THE OLD FOX DECEIV'D, *Martha Grimes*
65 SIX NUNS AND A SHOTGUN, *Colin Watson*

A Scene Of The Crime® Mystery

DEATH and the PRINCESS

Robert Barnard

A DELL BOOK

Published by
Dell Publishing Co., Inc.
1 Dag Hammarskjold Plaza
New York, New York 10017

ISBN: 0-440-12153-1

Reprinted by arrangement with Charles Scribner's Sons
Printed in the United States of America
First Dell printing—November 1983

DEATH
and the
PRINCESS

CONTENTS

CHAPTER 1

Royal Summons

The story of my intimate association with Royalty begins on a January day in 198– .

Does that sound like a passage from the ghastly memoirs of some Edwardian gaiety girl, long past gaiety or anything else except mendacity? Well, my association with royalty wasn't like that at all. You might say, I suppose, that the Princess brought a touch of glamour into my humdrum life. You might even say I brought a whiff of excitement into *her* humdrum life. But both these formulations are a bit too positive, compared with what actually happened.

Anyway, on the day in question I was lingering over a last cup of breakfast tea with Jan, my wife, and Daniel, my small son. They were shortly to return to Newcastle, where my wife is studying Arabic (for reasons that have never been entirely clear to me). I had nothing particular bothering me in the way of cases: about the only thing I was engaged on at the time was a leakage of classified information about welfare payments from a social security office. Cases do not come more tedious than that. Nevertheless, it was at that breakfast table that my life was invaded by royalty – though admittedly by minuscule royalty. The invasion signalled itself in the form of a ringing phone.

'Perry Trethowan,' I said.

'Hello, Perry,' said the gravelly voice of my superior, Joe Grierley, the Deputy Assistant Commissioner, 'I've got a job for you.'

'I've got one already,' I said. 'I'm supposed to be

finding a Mole in the Shoreditch Social Security Office. Feeding classified information about benefits to the *New Statesman*.'

'Forget it. You're going up in the world, Perry. I picked you specially, because you're couth.'

'I am not couth,' I protested. 'And I do not like cases that involve noble families.' (The last upper-crust family I'd been criminally involved with had been my own.)

'Noble families? Who said anything about noble families? We can do better than that. You are going to be personal bodyguard to the Princess Helena. No less.'

'No less?' I burst out. 'No more? might be a better question. What sort of a job is that for a man of my seniority?' I'd just been made Superintendent, and didn't at all fancy spending hours and hours attending charity matinées, royal tours of ball-bearing factories, and Girl Guide jamborees. 'Surely you can find someone else?' I pleaded. 'Couthness can't be in that short supply.'

'Couthness is as rare as muffins,' said Joe. 'And as you will realize when you think about it, I wouldn't have put you down for this without a reason. I'm putting you on with Joplin, who can do most of the charity matinée stuff. You are to have general responsibility for security. I'll see you this afternoon, and put you into the picture about the whys and wherefores.'

I was slightly mollified. The thought of sitting in limousines making well-bred conversation about the weather had caused me to jump the gun a bit. I said with a sigh of acquiescence: 'OK then, if I must. How do I address her, by the way?'

'Your Royal Highness first off, and then Ma'am,' said Joe. 'Pronounced Marm. I know all about it. I once did the same for Princess Anne.'

'Really? What was she like?'

'Screaming blue murder most of the time, and wetting her nappies. It was a while ago.'

'Well, at least mine is out of that stage,' I said.

'Oh yes, yours is out of that stage. If we could keep her in a playpen all day, things would be a lot easier. I'll send Joplin and a car round to your flat at ten—right?'

'I suppose so. Plain clothes?'

'Uniform. And make damn sure it's impeccable.'

So there were me and Jan spending the time until ten o'clock brushing hair and dandruff off my uniform and cleaning shoes to the sort of spit-and-polish brightness I remembered from my army days. At least that's the sort of work you can talk over, and we spent the time dredging up all we knew about the Princess Helena.

'She's absolutely *gorgeous*,' said Jan, with more than a suggestion of impending suspicion in her eye.

And the fact is, gorgeous she was, and this was what everybody knew about her. She had started doing the odd royal chore about three years before, when she was barely out of her 'teens. The press had been enraptured, scenting limitless fodder, and the young lady had become patron of this, honorary president of that, until very soon she was taken on to the royal strength, with a nice little sum on the Civil List and apartments in Kensington Palace, which one gathers is the regular doss-house for minor royals.

Her connection with the Royal Family was not particularly close. She was the daughter of the Princess Charlotte, who was the daughter of—well, I forget who, but I think it went back to George V, or Edward VII or someone. Princess Charlotte had been mildly notorious in her time: a royal high-liver about whom risqué stories were told at cocktail parties, songs were sung at hunt balls. Not that there was ever anything much said publicly. Luckily her heyday had been in the post-war years and the 'fifties, when, if you remember, anyone who said anything faintly critical of the Queen was run through with middle-class umbrellas in public places, and burned in effigy by Bishops in their Cathedral Closes. So there was never much in the newspapers and tattle-sheets, but—as I say—the whisper did get around. Jokes. Her name didn't help . . .

Well, Charlotte had married a German princeling with a name as long as your arm some time in the late 'fifties, had produced the undoubtedly gorgeous little Helena, and had then divorced in a blaze of publicity. By now it was the 'sixties, the age of *Private Eye*, and royalty was no longer wrapped in jewellers' cotton-wool, or stuck up for worship on a side-altar. Long before the decade ended she had driven her sports car over a cliff in Sardinia, taking with her a highly unsuitable escort and an amount of alcohol and drugs unusual even for Italy. A lot of *dolce vite* ended roughly the same way at that time.

So my little lady was brought up very quietly in the country by other exceedingly obscure offshoots of royalty. I suspect they may have been scared of something hereditary coming out in her: they sent her to a ridiculously decorous girls' school, the sort which seems to aim to turn out dowagers. Still, it seemed from what one read that they had not quite managed to snuff out that hereditary spark.

'I wish I wasn't going back to Newcastle at the end of the week,' said Jan.

'Why?' I asked. 'Don't you trust me?'

'Not absolutely altogether,' she said.

'Come off it. Princesses don't bed down with their police bodyguards,' I said.

'I bet her mother did,' said Jan, and I didn't feel like taking her up on that. 'But it's not so much that I want to keep an eye on you,' she went on (why is one always insulted when one's wife says things like that?). 'I want to hear all the details. What the apartments are like. What she wears. What she eats. Who she's going with. Particularly that. It's not often you get a chance of absolutely reliable inside gossip about the Royals. It's usually "I know a chap who knows a girl who knows another girl . . ." '

'You,' I said, 'are a thundering, old-fashioned, arse-licking snob.'

'I don't know where you get that idea,' said Jan, who did.

Then the car came, and I marched off to my date with the Royal Family—spick and span, resplendent, the very model of a modern police superintendent. Joplin was in the car already, and we went over the day's security arrangements and some of the general do's and don't's about protecting royal personages, about which he had been thoroughly briefed at the Yard. Joplin's about twenty-two, and a marvellous bloke to work with. He looks stolid, sensible, even a bit thick in a pleasant kind of way—until you notice his eyes. Then you realize there isn't a thing that he misses, not a detail. Those little London peepers are darting everywhere. He not only picks up everything that's said, he photographs the scene while he's listening, so that he can reproduce it for you afterwards, down to the tiniest detail. A marvellous young man, Joplin.

We got to Kensington Palace in a matter of minutes, or so it seemed. The driver, well-briefed, took us round to a discreet side-entrance, overlooking a street of embassies, and I took in a brief impression of a solid, comfortable Bill-and-Mary sort of pile while I talked to Joplin and sent him off to natter with the regular bobbies around the place. I myself was looked for, and met, very smoothly; then I was dribbled from flunkey to flunkey, like a genteel football, until finally I landed up in what must have been some kind of antechamber—mostly dark wood, with a peeling ceiling and a lot of musty greens and faded golds—and talking to a lady in her nondescript thirties. She had 'lady' written all over her, and was apparently 'in waiting' to boot. She was rather prim, severe, even repressed, and would have seemed rather an odd companion for the Princess Helena, had it not struck me that she could have been chosen either by the young lady herself, to provide piquant contrast, or by Someone Higher, to act as a watchdog.

'Her Royal Highness will see you at once,' she said, in the sort of flat upper-class voice I like least, replete with frigidity and effort. She went on, as if screwing the words out, and forcing an appearance of amiability: 'She always likes to meet new members of her security guard. But she has to leave for a luncheon engagement at eleven-thirty. I may have to interrupt you. She has very little idea of time.'

'Worrying,' I said.

She looked at me frostily, blinked, and led the way forward. I walked behind her, wondering idiotically whether there was any etiquette about room-entering that I was too raw to know about, whether it was right foot first or something lunatic like that. And I was still thinking about that when I was formally (very!) introduced by the lady-in-waiting, who then drifted in a superior manner out of the room.

And so there we were, together. And she was breathtaking, she really was—every bit as gorgeous as the press spreads suggested. I suppose delectable is the word that sums it up. She had a wonderful little body, confidently carried, and the dress she was wearing, while in every way royal, decorous, and hideously expensive-looking, still seemed to cling provocatively at interesting places and tantalize you by new suggestions every time she moved. Her hair was dark, short, and beautifully modelled around her ears; her mouth was wide, her eyes were enormous, dark and sparkling. Oh, she was a pippin all right!

'Hello,' she said. And then she giggled. 'I say, aren't you *large*.'

The voice was a let-down, I had to admit. It was tinkling, trivial, more than a little silly. Possibly a voice for bed, but hell to hear over the breakfast-table.

'Yes, Your Royal Highness,' I said. 'I am generally considered too much of a good thing.'

She giggled again, delightedly. 'Oh, I didn't say that. Not at all. You're not a bit like your predecessor, you know.'

'My predecessor, Ma'am?'

'My personal bodyguard. I've had several of them, and some have been perfectly lovely. But McPhail was awfully dour.'

She pronounced it 'dower', but I knew what she meant. Inspector McPhail always looked as if he'd only spoken twelve words in the last week, and bitterly regretted six of them.

'Yes, McPhail does seem to take the idea of the Silent Service a bit far,' I said. 'Ma'am.'

She giggled again. 'I'm glad you're not like him. Because I like somebody to talk to. My lady-in-waiting is perfectly sweet, of course, but terribly quiet. I like somebody with something to say for himself. I say, though, you're not an intellectual, are you?'

'No, Ma'am. I hardly have two ideas to rub together, most of the time.'

'Oh, I'm glad. Because I'm awfully stupid, really. I sometimes have dreadful difficulty with the speeches they give me.'

'Oh, does somebody write them for you, Ma'am?' I said.

'Of course. What did you think?'

I was leading up to saying that I thought royal speeches were written by computer, but instinct told me that would be going too far in the first five minutes of our acquaintanceship. Couth of you, Perry old chap! And the fact is, there was something about her, in spite of the giggling and the girlishness, that warned me off, told me there were borders not to be strayed over.

So I merely said: 'Silly of me, Ma'am. I should have realized.'

'They're all written out. Otherwise I should just stand up there and gape at them. I say, you wouldn't like to hear me say my speech for this afternoon, would you? I'm having lunch with Aid for the Elderly, and then I have to address the Annual General Meeting. And I *know* they'll have put some frightfully long words in it.'

'Of course, Ma'am, if you think it would help.'

'Oh, I *do*,' she said, looking at me with those eyes, those enormous eyes—dark, inviting, appealing eyes which had everything except intelligence. She blinked them with conscious provocation, then danced over to the desk.

'If you're with me for a long time,' she said, 'you'll get awfully used to speeches about the Old. The Old are rather my thing.'

Come to think about it, I had seen an awful lot of pictures of her visiting Twilight Homes—pictures of toothless old men mumbling speeches of loyalty and gratitude as they shook the royal paw. So the Royals specialized, did they? It seemed incongruous, at first, loading the delectable Helena with the burden of the national old age. On the other hand, she must obviously have brought dim, warm stirrings to innumerable aged loins the length and breadth of the country, happy reminders of remembered pleasures, vain hopes that all was not lost. So no doubt there was a grain of sense in it, and she did a lot of good in her way.

She picked up a couple of sheets of paper, on which I saw some very widely-spaced typing—to minimize the peering at a script, I supposed.

'It's awful bosh,' she said gaily, 'but you have to read it as if you *know* what it meant, even if you can't pretend you do actually *mean* it. Well, here goes.' She swallowed, and dived into the shallow waters of royal prose.

'It is a great pleasure to me to be present this afternoon at the Annual General Meeting of Aid for the Elderly. As your Patron, I have seen, in my travels up and down the country, the splendid work you do in providing retirement homes and special comforts for the not so young, those dignified and independent citizens who are in too many ways the forgotten members of our community. In their twilight years, old people need above all to maintain their independence and self-respect, and in this context the motto of our Society is both significant and inspiring: "Self-reliance where possible, help where necessary." We are all committed to this common gaol—'

'Goal,' I said.

'I beg your pardon?' She raised her eyes from her script with more than a touch of hauteur. *Not* a young lady, definitely, to step over the border with.

'I think, Ma'am, it should be "goal": "We are all committed to this common goal." '

She thought for a few seconds, and then giggled.

'Oh yes, I suppose it should. The way I said it sounds like some of the Old People's Homes I've visited. Aren't you clever! And you couldn't even see the script.'

She went back to her text and droned her way through it. It sounded like the collective wisdom of a Sunday School class from a particularly dim suburb of Bournemouth. Occasionally, however, it got more technical, and I was able to advise her on the pronunciation of 'gerontology'. She was awfully grateful, she said, because she must have been getting it wrong for years and no one had told her. At the end she was quite effusive.

'I can see we're going to get on *awfully* well,' she said. 'Most of the other policemen have been just that bit *stuffy*. I mean, always trying to *stop* one. I do think at my age you've got to have just a bit of freedom, don't you?'

She opened those enormous eyes still wider, in appeal.

'Well, yes,' I said. 'Now, in that connection, Ma'am—'

But we were interrupted by the lady-in-waiting. She knocked discreetly and entered in what must have been her characteristic way: silent, thin-lipped, fussy, disapproving.

'The car leaves in ten minutes, Your Royal Highness,' she drawled. 'One doesn't want to be late.'

One didn't mind in the least being late, I suspected, if one was the Princess Helena. There was something almost of petulance in her reaction.

'Oh dear, what a shame! Just when we were beginning to be friends. You're not coming with us, I suppose.'

'No, Ma'am. Sergeant Joplin will be with you today.'

'Is he nice?' She caught a look from her lady-in-waiting, and pouted still more. 'Well, I'm sure we'll have *lots* of opportunities in the future. I must fly!'

And she danced out, followed by her grey shadow. Within a matter of seconds a secretarial flunkey came in to show me out. I had the feeling of being caught up in an infinitely smooth-running piece of machinery, the ultimate in unobtrusive efficiency. Inside the Palace, the Princess was cocooned. But I did not get the impression she was a young lady who would be happy for long in a cocoon.

CHAPTER 2

The Loyal Subject

After my interview with the Princess Helena amid the tatty splendours of Kensington Palace, I mortified the flesh with a lunch of sausage and mash in the Scotland Yard canteen. I smothered the sausages with tomato ketchup and read the *Daily Grub*, and that way brought myself sufficiently down to earth for my interview with Joe Grierley. Joe may appreciate my couthness on occasion, but he can sniff out uppitiness like a monomaniacal beagle.

As I pushed back my chair to go up to Joe's office, I caught sight of the Princess herself on the *Grub*'s back page. She was in the rear of a gaggle of royals trooping in to a Royal film show – but she was the one the *Grub* pictured. She was looking very demure. The film sounded dire.

When I had settled myself comfortably into an arm-chair in Joe's office, prepared for a long talk, he looked at me roguishly.

'Enjoy yourself?' he said, in his gravelly, cockles-and-mussels voice.

'So-so,' I said. 'Not really my scene, however difficult you may find that to believe. Contrary to the received opinion around here, I did not have duchesses cooing over my cradle, or exiled royalty showering me with monogrammed christening-spoons.'

'You disappoint me,' said Joe, with a fruity chuckle. Joe has the figure for fruity chuckles, being a square, genial cockney who has run very much to tummy. He was born in Stepney, has one of the sharpest and fastest brains in the business, and a sense of humour too, though rather one of the breasts and buttocks variety. We get on well, but I know he thinks me cold and 'sarky'. It's true I never went much on seaside postcards.

'And what's your opinion of the young lady?' Joe asked.

'A corker,' I said. 'Which should be obvious to the bleariest old eye. Beyond that, I'm saying nothing till I have the whole story out of you. I presume something's in the air.'

'We're sniffing,' he admitted, 'and faintly rotten smells are being wafted to us over the winds. Otherwise, as I said, we wouldn't have landed this in your lap.'

'So I should hope,' I said, for I was not yet mollified. 'So I should bloody hope.'

'Now, now,' said Joe, settling down in his desk, the way he had when getting ready for a good old natter; 'it's a compliment in a way that we think you're up to it. Well now, do you remember old Snobby Driscoll?'

I let out a great burst of laughter, and immediately sat easier in my chair. 'Now you're getting more into my line of country! Do I remember Snobby Driscoll! Matter of fact, I sent him up for his most recent term.'

'Did you now? Get to know him at all?'

'Socially? Only the sort of acquaintanceship that is forged on a journey from Curzon Street to the Yard. Him not having the full use of his hands. We talked about the world situation, as far as I remember. He spent the time lamenting the fact that the country was no longer run by gentlemen.'

'That's old Snobby. Tory to the backbone.'

'A good old nineteenth-century patriot, that much I did gather. He'd do anything for his country except stop robbing the richer members of it. Said things had gone to the dogs since they abolished hanging. It gave the whole trip a weird sense of unreality. They don't breed 'em like that anymore – a real character, in a ghastly sort of way. What in God's name has Snobby got to do with all this? You said *did* I remember? . . .'

'Right. Gone to meet the Eternal Lord Chief Justice. Died in Brixton, matter of three weeks ago.'

'And thereby, I suppose, hangs a tale.'

'Maybe. And there again, maybe not. But one thing's for sure, we can't take any chances over this one. Well now, he may not have got on to it during your little drive, but among his other foibles he was devoted to the Royal Family.'

'Figures.'

'Yes—but this was a real passionate thing. Dated from the war. He was an East Ender, of course, and they were bombed . . .'

'I get you. The Queen Mum came visiting and flapped a friendly boa in his direction.'

'You've got it in one. She was Queen then, of course. She took a cuppa with his old mum, and had a cosy jaw about her sons in Parkhurst, Broadmoor and the Colchester glasshouse. Since then Snobby was to be seen at any Royal occasion he happened to be out for, cheering like crazy and waving five or six Union Jacks.'

'They don't,' I said again, 'make 'em like that any-more. Well, what's the score? Don't tell me he left his hoard of upper-crust loot to little Princess Helena.'

'I don't think Snobby would have thought that quite the thing. No, what happened was that as he was dying—it was cancer, by the by, and he was drugged, but as far as we can gather he was entirely *compos mentis*—he sent for the Governor, told the orderlies he wanted to give him an important message.'

'I'm getting the same sense of unreality I had on that car ride back to the Yard.'

'Point taken. I had the same reaction myself. Well, what old Snobby said was: "Tell them to take care of Princess Helena. There's something up. Something nasty. Tell them they've got to keep an eye on her." '

'End of message? Normal service will not be resumed?'

'Pretty much so. The Governor tried to get more out of him, but it was no go. Snobby wasn't one to grass as a general rule, and they don't trust the governors these days like they used to trust the old brigade. They know they're just Home Office stooges.'

'Well,' I said, not overly impressed, 'it's a pretty thin tale as it stands. What was it supposed to be about? Some kind of terrorist plot?'

'That was our first thought: the IRA, or one of the

People's Armies for the liberation of the suffering masses, whether they like it or not. And naturally we doubled the security, as unobtrusively as we could. Still, when we came to think it over, it didn't seem likely. What kind of connection could there have been between the IRA and old Snobby Driscoll? If he'd had his way the buggers would never have been given Home Rule. Same with your Red Army mob. Snobby wouldn't have let one of them so much as mind his jemmy. He had firm principles about mixing politics and crime—especially their politics. We've been chewing it over, and I've had a bit of a natter with the Commissioner, and we've come to the conclusion that it's something else. In other words, it's got to be something much closer to Snobby's line of country.'

I relaxed a bit in my chair again. 'Well, at least that takes the heat off us a bit, doesn't it? If it's not a question of a death threat.'

'I didn't quite say that.'

'Oh God. You mean I'm there to prevent someone being killed?'

'I think someone may already have been.'

I sighed. 'OK, give me the gen.'

But Joe didn't seem to want to come straight out with the story. He settled himself over his desk in a Buddha-like pose, not looking too happy, like most Buddhas. 'In good time, Perry. But first of all, what's your impression of the little lady herself?'

'Come off it, Joe. I only saw her for a quarter of an hour or so. She read me her speech for Save the Senile, or some such bunch of do-gooders. What sort of impression of Her Madge do you get when you see her reading the Speech from the Throne?'

'Knowing you, Perry, you formed a judgement, snap or otherwise. What was it?'

I shrugged. 'Gorgeous to look at. Gorgeous body. Knows it. Probably uses it. Do you know a word that the

French have, or used to have: "une cocktease"?'

'Does that mean what it sounds like?'

'Yes.'

'Is that what you think she is?'

'Yes. Whether wittingly or unwittingly I wouldn't like to say.'

'Would you think she sleeps around?'

I considered. 'Well, hazarding a guess, I'd say *no*. Sleeps *with*, now and again, yes. But sleeps *around*, no. She's got a fair sense of her position. Why don't you ask McPhail?'

'You're not suggesting—?'

'No, of course not. That would have been offering rump steak to a vegetarian. I merely meant he ought to know.'

'Well, I did ask. In so far as I got anything out of him at all, he agreed with you. Now and again, without a doubt, and perhaps fairly regularly with one or two, but certainly no nympho. Still, the fact is, she's got any number of young men sniffing round her skirts.'

'So the newspapers imply.'

'If she had been sleeping regularly with any one of them, that might have been as good a point of departure for us as any. Blackmail, sensational serials in the *Sunday Gutter*—you know the kind of stuff. Then we might conceivably have found some kind of criminal connection that led us back to Snobby Driscoll. But the fact is, we can't pick on any one of them. It's a nightmare, because there are so many. As far as collecting casual companions is concerned, the young lady is not discriminating. In fact, she's bloody unwise.'

'Oh? Who is there, then?'

'Well, for a start, there's an MP.'

'That shouldn't matter, surely, provided he's of the right party?'

'He's of the wrong party. And he's way to the left of

it—used to be a cheer-leader for Wedgwood-Benn, now branching out with ambitions of his own. Even worse, the man used to be a card-carrying Communist.'

I never understand why to people of Joe's generation Communists are always card-carrying. Do they go around with them clutched in their little hot hands?

'When was that?' I asked.

'At Oxford.'

'Everyone at Oxford joins the Communist Party. I believe you sign up when you join the Oxford Union. Denis Healey was a Communist at Oxford. If it had been Cambridge we might have got worried.'

Joe grunted. 'Then there's another of her escorts, if that's the word, who's an actor. Name of Jeremy Styles.'

'I know him. Of him, at least. Opened in the new Simeon Black play last week.'

'That's the boy. Done a lot of television work as well—used in those classic serials because he looks well in costume. But *not*, as far as we can see, safe. And then there's the Honourable Edwin Robert Montague Frere.'

'At least it sounds as if he's the right class.'

'Hmmm. He's that all right. He's pretty as a puma, and about as safe. His father is the Earl of Leamington. The Honourable Edwin (who the hell thought up that title?) is to be seen most nights hanging around the tables at the Wellington Casino, in Park Lane. In dire need of the necessary, that lad.'

'Like most younger sons of peers. Like most of the elder ones too, come to that. I'd have thought you'd only hang around casinos if you had money to lose rather than if you were in need.'

'He's in need *because* he loses money. Very often he watches more than plays. Fascinated. And he leeches on to people.'

'Charming. Is that the lot?'

'By no means. I'll give you the list, with what notes

we've been able to get together on them. It's quite a collection. Even, God help us, a footballer.'

'Not George B—'

'I said a footballer. Anyway, he's a bit out of her age-range. She mostly goes for men in their twenties. Now, the fact is, there are limits to how far we can fence the young lady in.'

'I'll bet.'

'No, I'm not being snide, Perry. She's a young thing, and naturally she wants her fling. Works hard for it too, as far as I can gather: does a lot of the fairly depressing jobs the other Royals won't touch. She's got to have her fun, and her freedom, and we've got to make sure she has hundred per cent protection. And that's the devil of it: the two just don't go together.'

'That's for sure.'

'The only thing I can think of is to go to her, put it to her: tell her what I've told you, tell her to keep her eyes open, tell her to report to us everything, but *everything*, that happens that's just that bit out of the ordinary. Tell us where she's going, so we can case it in advance. Tell us who she's going with, where she might possibly go on afterwards. In other words, rely on her good sense and get her co-operation, down to the last detail.'

I thought for a bit: 'There's just one thing you haven't taken account of in that scenario of yours.'

'What's that?'

'She hasn't got a brain in her head.'

Joe looked disappointed. 'Think not?'

'Not on the surface, anyway. Unless it's a front, part of the cocktease act. If it was for real, she could blab the whole thing to any of those young men she goes with. And I imagine absolute discretion is the first order of the day?'

'Oh absolutely,' Joe said, worried stiff. 'You think it might be more danger than it's worth?'

'I do. Now, come on, Joe: you're still holding out on

me. What was that about a death?'

'Ah yes. You'll have to know about that. But it's all pretty nebulous. The fact is, while we've been doing this double-quick investigation of her young men these last few weeks, we've turned up the name of William Tredgold a couple of times. Bill Tredgold everyone knew him as.'

I wrinkled my forehead. 'Never heard of him. Should I have?'

'No. He was a reporter. Unwise again, you see. He worked for the *Birmingham Standard*. Was up for a job with the *Guardian*. Roly-poly sort of chap, from his pictures, but attractive in a scruffy-puppy sort of a way. She went around with him for two or three weeks. Went to several rather dubious parties with him while she was doing a round of charity openings and suchlike in the Midlands. Very possibly slept with him, in his flat in Solihull.'

'I like the idea of Royalty getting to know how the other half sleeps.'

'You won't by the time you've finished this job. Anyway, the affair seems to have fizzled out, if it ever was much of one. But the fact is, the young man died . . .'

'I see. How?'

'He was staying at one of these genuine Elizabethan bash-your-head-on-a-beam kind of inns, at a place called Knightley, in Shropshire. Rooms heated by gas. Seems he left the fire on when he went to bed. There must have been a fault in it: flame went out, gas stayed on, consequences just what you'd guess. Verdict of accidental death.'

'Hmmm. I see.'

'Windows shut tight. Nothing against that. It was early December. But his mother says he *never* slept with the window shut.'

'Yes. Go on.'

'He'd been drinking before he went to sleep. Bottle of white wine. Nothing against that. But there were white wine glasses there, and a tray. And yet the hotel had no record of any order for it.'

'I see. Fixed in any way?'

'By the time we got around to looking into it, the case was dead. Evidence destroyed.'

'Yes, of course. Anything else?'

'One thing. He wasn't alone. There was a girl with him.'

'She died too?'

'Oh yes. Both of them dead as doornails in the morning. The trouble is—'

'Yes?'

'Well, there was nothing close, you understand, but the fact is, that this girl . . . just vaguely . . . rather resembled the Princess Helena. Get me?'

I got him.

CHAPTER 3

Flunkeydom

So there it was. We sat about for some time, Joe and I, talking over the various alternative possibilities. They amounted, in essence, to these: that the deaths were indeed accidental, as the inquest had decided; that someone had wanted to kill either Bill Tredgold, or his girl-friend, or both; or that someone had intended to kill the Princess Helena. We had to admit that, abstractly considered, the last seemed by far the most likely.

In the end we got down to brass tacks, and I made various suggestions about security: that my job should be duplicated, so that when I was busy on the case, the

Princess Helena's routine security would be in good hands. I suggested a chief inspector who was both competent and personable, to keep the Princess happy as well as safe. I suggested doubling Joplin's position too, and said I'd say more about routine security at the Palace when I knew more about the current arrangements. Then I went off with the dossier Joe and his men had made about the affair so far.

I settled down to it in my own office, feet up amid its rather bleak but familiar comforts. What the dossier amounted to, in fact, was a record of the Princess's 'off-duty' engagements, with details of, and an assessment of, the young men she had recently been going around with. I felt she had been getting more private life than we are usually told royalty is able to manage, but of course, for all I knew, much of what I was learning would have been commonplace to readers of Nigel Dempster or Lady Olga Maitland. My own family had provided too much fodder for gossip columnists for me to get much enjoyment out of them. I felt rather shabby, going through all this intimate stuff, like some sort of dating-service adviser, or a second-degree pimp. No doubt the feeling was going to grow in the course of the case. For as long as there seemed to be a threat against the Princess, the poor girl was going to have no private life, whether she knew it or not. Unless, of course, she twigged, and outwitted us. Quite dim-witted people can be very sharp in matters that affect them personally, and it was on the cards that she would get wise to any additional security we devised, and give it the slip. If she did, she could well sign her own death-warrant.

Anyway, they were a right bunch, her boy-friends, to my way of thinking. I'll give you the details on them when you meet them, but there was hardly a one of them I'd trust with my old granny's last sixpence, apart from Bill Tredgold, and he was dead. All of them would have to be talked to, sized up, thoroughly gone into. The question at the moment was, what approach was I to use? If I was completely open and interviewed them in my official capacity, then the case was wide open, with newspaper headlines—the lot. With ten or twelve names on my dossier, you could be quite certain one of them would pocket Fleet Street Danegeld and blab. One thing I've had more than enough of is cases that hit the headlines.

My mind honed in on the Honourable Edwin Robert Montague Frere. The nightly frequenter of casinos. Mostly to be seen, if the dossier was to be believed, hanging over the roulette wheel in the Wellington Club, panting at the restrictions that indigence imposes.

Now, anyone can go to a casino. Policemen went, in their private capacity, to casinos (though *not*, I may add, any policeman of whom I had any opinion at all). It seemed a good enough starting-point, while I worked out a plan of campaign for the rest of the desirable Helena's male harem. The fact that the Wellington was a club would not, I suspected, present insuperable difficulties. I found the number in the book, and asked the discreet voice on the other end of the line about membership.

'Your name, sir?'

'Leopold Trethowan,' I said, feeling that discretion was the better part of honesty. I slurred the surname, hoping it would be heard as Tregorran.

'That will be perfectly all right, sir. When were you thinking of coming along?'

'I thought perhaps tonight . . .'

'Splendid, sir. I'll have your membership card ready for you.'

How easy. How wonderfully, illegally easy!

Meanwhile there were still many hours before the wheels would be spinning at the Wellington Club. I decided to make a return visit to Kensington Palace and check up on the behind-the-scenes security. As I expected, it was tip-top, but I enjoyed nosing around the palace and its surroundings, I noted without joy the proximity of the public touring the open areas of the place, and finally I made one or two suggestions aimed at meeting the special situation we were in at the moment. While I was talking to the man in charge of general palace security the royal limousine drove by, with Sergeant Joplin in the front seat, and when the ladies had disappeared inside in a flurry of *haute couture* I went over and had a word with him.

'Have a nice day?'

'Boring as hell,' Garry Joplin said. 'I don't know how she sits through it and keeps looking interested. Gave me the screaming ab-dabs. The lunch was all right, I suppose.'

'Better than meals-on-wheels, I imagine. What about the people, though?'

'Nothing of interest for us, I'd say. Nice enough lot, mostly middle-aged or elderly themselves. Hard-working, do a lot of good—you know the type. Hardly what we're after.'

'No—except we don't really know what we are after. Nothing else out of the ordinary—no accidents on the way?'

'Not a thing.'

'What about the lady-in-waiting?'

'Stuffy bitch. What do you mean, what about her?'

'Does she keep her eyes open, keep close, do her job?'

'Oh yes, like a well-dressed leech. Close, but yet in the background, if you get me. Drops the odd genteel platitude here and there, but mostly stays mum and keeps her eyes open. She relaxed a bit when it came to the private bit.'

'Private bit?'

'Just the committee, for cocktails before lunch. Just ten or twelve of the top nobs. I hung around, of course, not getting offered a shot myself. They all stood up clutching their grog and making well-bred conversation about the weather. One of the do-gooders was a noble relative of Lady Muck the train-bearer, and she had a bit of a jaw with him. Otherwise she's been at the lass's side all the time, passing the sort of remarks you get in language primers. Fun for the little girl!'

'Cramped your style, Garry, I can see that. Never mind. If I know the young lady she'll get on friendly terms before many days are out. I thought I might go and have a word with the secretary johnnie—coming along?'

'Might as well,' said Sergeant Joplin, and we had a word with a flunkey and found ourselves shunted forward on the conveyor-belt of flunkeydom until finally we found ourselves ushered into a rather raggedly splendid office—large, ornate, sparsely furnished, and cold as charity. A dowdy secretary typed at a side table miles from anywhere, and intoned that Mr Brudenell would be in in a moment. She motioned us to two upright chairs, eighteenth-century jobs, seemingly designed for midgets with spinal problems. We stood and waited.

Two minutes, and in bustled Mr James Brudenell, private secretary to the Princess Helena. I suspected he liked bustling in on people, and had probably only been in the next room anyway, watering the aspidistras. He was a pouter-pigeon little man, oh-so-smart in his morning coat and trimmings, but with a fat little tummy which he thrust self-importantly before him, as if he were pregnant with a new generation of private secretaries to royalty. He had weak little eyes behind strong glasses, and a thin veneer of geniality covering a solid wedge of self-importance and conceit. I didn't greatly take to him, as you'll have gathered.

'Ah, Superintendent Trethowan,' he enthused, shaking my hand with a white, plump collection of fingers and palm. He ignored Joplin and motioned us to sit, a balancing act we gingerly performed.

'Good to meet you, have a little chat,' he went on. 'I of course know you by reputation . . . Read about the death of your father . . .'

Oh Mr Brudenell, you did start out on the wrong foot!

'Oh yes?' I said, chilly.

'Most unfortunate . . . Still, even in the best families.'

No one knew better than I that mine was not one of the best families. 'I wonder if we might have a few words about this security angle?' I said.

'Of course, of course. We're in your hands. The general lines, as you will know, are laid down from the Palace for all members of the Royal Family in the public eye. You don't perceive any obvious *lacuna*, I hope?'

'No *lacunæ* have become evident to me as yet,' I said, and saw a laugh waft through Garry Joplin's eyes. 'On the other hand, the Princess, being young, and no doubt wanting a good time, does present problems . . .'

'You think so?' said James Brudenell. 'Not unusual ones, surely? All members of the Royal Family have to enjoy some sort of private life. And they do. Quite notably so, in some cases . . .'

'Yes, of course,' I said. 'But no doubt with the older members that private life has acquired—how shall I put it?—a certain pattern. They have formed a circle, or perhaps several distinct circles. That's quite manageable. But what we are worried about with the Princess Helena is that—naturally at her age—she is making new friends all the time. The circle, if I may put it like that, is very, very fluid.'

'Hmm, yes, I see,' said Mr Brudenell, screwing his rather piggy little face into thought. 'You said "worried", Superintendent. Was that just a chance word, or is there any special reason to be worried, eh?'

I took an instantaneous decision. 'Oh, no special reason at all,' I said. I had no doubt that Mr James Brudenell was one hundred per cent trustworthy, a twenty-four-carat soul, like all royal servants, but the fact was I didn't like him, and I'm afraid that meant I didn't feel like trusting him. 'Put me down as a new broom, wanting to sweep cleaner than all the old brooms. But as you must realize, we are bound to look at the way the Princess spends her spare time. Nothing censorious, you understand—mere common prudence. And I must say that her escorts have been—what shall I say?—a fairly assorted bunch.'

Mr Brudenell snuffled. This seemed to be a subject after his own heart. 'A point you are very well qualified to appreciate, Superintendent,' he purred, gentleman to gentleman. 'But what have you? We live in a democratic age, more's the—well! And of course one has to say that the Princess's . . . openness—in social matters I mean—does her no harm with the Press.'

'No-o-o,' I said. 'Tell me, is there any of her escorts that you personally have felt uneasy about?'

'For a time there was a footballer!' Mr Brudenell wailed. 'And she's still seeing this actor fellow, I know that. There was a journalist—can you imagine anything more unwise?—but he died, thank God. And then there's this Bayle, the Labour MP. When you *think* what some members of his party say about the Civil List!'

I had the feeling that Mr Brudenell's feelings of unease were on social rather than personal grounds.

'Any more?' I asked.

'Oh dear, no one special, but she goes to *parties*, you know, and meets up with all sorts. You see my problem: now the Princess is "one of the team", so to speak, with a regular round of engagements, the *one* thing we are anxious to avoid is the wrong sort of publicity!'

'Certainly I see your problem,' I said coolly. That wasn't my problem. 'What about the Hon. Edwin Frere? Hasn't she been seeing a good deal of him?'

He looked at me wide-eyed. 'But I don't see any

problem there. I can personally vouch that it's an excellent family. His grandfather was Bearer of the Footstool at the last coronation but one!'

'I'm sure the family is absolutely tip-top,' I said. 'But as you said a moment ago, even in the best of them . . . I heard something about gambling debts.'

'Wild oats,' said Mr Brudenell indulgently. 'Sort of thing no one would even have thought it worth mentioning fifty years ago. Of course the family's not well off. You may remember they had to sell a really exquisite Dürer when his father inherited. Bought by a German industrialist. Appalling to think of the country's artistic heritage being dissipated in that way! No doubt the young man feels the pinch, like so many.'

'So as far as you are concerned there is no problem in that direction? . . . Well, no doubt you're right. What would you say was the pattern of the Princess's social life—I mean her private social life, away from her official duties?'

Mr Brudenell sighed again, and tut-tutted. 'Well, there, of course, I'm not really involved, officially involved, that is. But as you say it is all rather uncontrolled. She goes to parties, meets people, they ask her out—to clubs, houseparties or whatever—she meets more people, and so it goes on. And I needn't tell you how horribly mixed up everything has become in the world of today. I mean *socially* mixed up. Men of quite good family, hobnobbing with *all sorts*. And they do all *kinds* of jobs!' He suddenly put his hand over his mouth. 'Oh, I do beg your pardon!'

'Granted,' I said. 'What it all boils down to is that there must be an awful lot that the Princess gets up to—sorry, I can't think of a more appropriate phrase—that you know little or nothing about.'

'Quite. Quite. A very great deal.'

'Or her lady-in-waiting either.'

'Certainly. Lady Dorothy can hardly be expected to be on duty twenty-four hours a day. Nor, I may say, would she *wish* to go to many of the places the Princess might frequent. A lady-in-waiting is the attendant for official occasions, nothing more.'

'Naturally,' I said. I got a very strange sense that Mr Brudenell considered Lady Dorothy Whateverhername was a lady, but that he wasn't too sure about the Princess. 'Presumably what you are concerned with mainly is the Princess's public role—'

'Precisely.'

'Who she meets, what she does on official occasions?'

'Exactly. We choose the sort of function she may grace, the sort of body she may become patron of, even on occasion the people she may be asked to meet at these functions.'

'I see. It sounds like a delicate business. Could you give me some idea of how you would go about it?'

He gestured expansively. 'It's an enormous question, Superintendent. *Awfully* delicate, as you say. Much of it is done at the Palace itself. Let's—*greatly* over-simplifying—take functions. Say a garden party. Now, say it was a political garden party—in aid of Conservative Party funds. Quite out of the question. Say it was in aid of a fund to buy Disraeli's birthplace. Possible, but needs to be looked at closely, to check on local political involvement, and so on. Say it's a charitable function: look at the charity, see if there are any controversial implications. Say it's a police garden party: generally acceptable, but the Police can acquire political overtones in certain circumstances. Is it an area where there have been—hmmm, you'll pardon me, I do hope—accusations of corruption, recently? Or brutality? Is there a controversial Chief Constable? They can sail very close to the political. In that case, we regretfully refuse, if you take my point.'

'Yes, I see. Clearly the whole thing rests on a knife edge. Now, about people—'

But at that point we were interrupted by a flunkey. A tall, fair-haired young man in the local uniform entered the room, and in a hushed voice, like an atheist in Canterbury Cathedral, informed Mr Brudenell that the Princess would like to see him in connection with her engagement of tomorrow morning. It was a splendid opportunity to bustle out, and Brudenell bustled, his fat little arse waggling behind him. Joplin and I escaped into the open air, escorted every inch of the way by the flunkey. I tried to make conversation with him, but he put me frostily in my place, as if he were editor of *The Times* and I was a delivery boy. Outside the air was cold, but it felt warmer than inside.

'Well,' I said to Joplin, 'how do you like mingling with the Great? Notice anything about Brudenell?'

'Homosexual, nervous, full of himself, probably having it off with the footman,' said Joplin.

'Really?' I said. 'How did you get that last bit?'

'Just a look he gave him as he went out. Otherwise, of course, a creep and a snob, as I suppose you'd agree, sir.'

'Of the worst. I agree about the "nervous" bit too, and that worries me. I must say, when I came this morning I felt I was witnessing the performance of the perfect machine—the human equivalent of a Rolls-Royce. Now, after talking to Brudenell, I'm not so sure.'

And that feeling stayed with me as I went back to the flat, ate a hurriedly grilled steak, played a moderately straight bat to all Jan's questions, and tried to satisfy Daniel as to what a real-life Princess looked like. Daniel gave up after a time, because really he's more interested in elephants and badgers, but not so Jan. She remained with me while I bathed and donned my best bib and tucker, and she questioned and prodded, alternately lapping it up and boggling. She didn't believe me when I said I thought the lady was stupid, did believe me when I said I thought she was gorgeous, believed me when I described the army of flunkies, didn't believe me when I said the palace was tatty. Finally I was ready for my evening's excursion. She brushed me down, straightened my tie and suggested that I take a taxi.

'Why shouldn't I drive there?'

'What, and arrive at the Wellington Club in a 1971 Morris 1100?' she said.

I saw her point, and rang the nearest taxi-rank. As we stood waiting at the door Jan said, 'I'll be up when you get back' – but that I could have guessed anyway.

CHAPTER 4

Young Blades

The Wellington Club was situated five minutes or so from Apsley House, but I doubted whether it had more than a nominal and opportunistic connection with the Iron Duke. It was in a quiet street just off Park Lane, and its existence was signalled by the discreetest of plaques by its front door. It had a very grand doorman, dressed in plushy brown with gold buttons, but when you peered beneath the top hat you saw that he was youngish, and tough.

It took no more than a couple of minutes to get through the formalities – if that is the word for the laughable process which gave me a membership card and admittance to these Regency splendours for life, supposing they were never so indiscreet as to get closed down. I was led upstairs by the Secretary, a slippery middle-aged man with exquisite manners and a gutless voice adept at uttering nothings. We came to what were clearly the first floors of two or three adjacent houses, knocked together to make a series of rooms dedicated to the businesses of gambling, drinking and eating. The biggest of the rooms held the roulette tables, and the most glittering crowd; through an arch at the far end were smaller rooms, not so well lit, and there people were sitting around small tables with cards in their hands. At the far end, cut off from the main rooms, was something that seemed to be the dining-room, and to the right of the roulette tables was the bar. The dining-room did not look too popular, but the bar was. People gravitated with glasses from it to the tables: old men with red eyes and bulging moustaches; middle-aged women in pink frills, with lots of back and bosom; young men in dinner-suits that fitted, with reddening faces and eyes either cold or hungry. Casinos, I suspect, are not places you should go to if you feel an urgent desire to love your fellow creatures.

'Do you see anyone you know?' enquired the Secretary.

'I've no doubt I shall,' I lied. 'Please don't let me keep you. I'll have a drink and watch for a bit.'

I really didn't have much choice. The price of my brandy set me back so much that I lost any vestigal desire I might have had to chuck away my well-earned dibs at the tables. I had, it is true, a wallet stuffed full of notes, but this was for purposes of verisimilitude; the money came from Scotland Yard, and emphatically had to go back there next morning. I held my glass in my hand at chest level, as I'd seen them do in *Tatler* advertisements, and strolled over to watch the fun.

Or rather to watch the people. Because if you're not absolutely fascinated by gambling you soon lose interest in the processes of winning and losing, and start watching the gamblers instead—the varieties of pleasure registered by the ones who win, the gradations of greed, frustration, bitterness and rage in the faces of the ones who lose.

Casinos might have been invented, I thought, to illustrate the step-by-step pathway to Hell. Certainly there were lost souls there, and ones so gay and insouciant that you could almost miss seeing the gaping pit at their feet. The croupiers were quick, dexterous and funny. Nobody much laughed. I looked around me casually, ignoring the red, thirsty, middle-aged faces, and the high-spirited young women. I scanned the young men: the guards officers, the tyros from the City, the rising lawyers, the congenitally idle. Finally I felt sure I had my man, the one whose photograph I had seen in Joe's dossier. There he was hovering restlessly round the outer fringes of the various groups: he was tall, fretful, handsome, with a lock of hair falling over cold blue eyes; he had a ski-slope nose and a petulant mouth, and he looked at the tables with a yearning, hungry expression, as if he had arrived at the gates of Paradise five minutes after closing time. Disraeli lamented that selling one's soul to the Devil had gone out of fashion, because it was such a useful custom for the younger sons of peers. Certainly Edwin Frere looked willing to consider a good offer.

When he pulled himself away, with palpable effort, from the crowd around the tables, and swanned it over to the bar, I downed my brandy and wandered over after him. The bar stools had ugly legs, twisting outwards, and I managed a fairly convincing stumble over one, and knocked his arm just as he was putting his glass down on the bar top.

'Oh, I say, I'm most frightfully sorry,' I said. (Do people talk like that still, I wondered?) 'Have I spilt it? Awfully clumsy of me. Do let me buy you another.'

'No harm done,' said the Honourable Edwin Frere. 'Thanks.'

He named the sort of malt whisky I thought twice about buying even at Christmas, and I named a better brandy than I'd had first time round. I noticed the barman shoot me a sharp glance. I think he put me down as a shyster on the make, and probably thought that I'd chosen a bloody bad victim. We settled ourselves against the bar, gazing over to the roulette room as if it were the Elysian Fields.

'Haven't seen you here before, have I?' said Frere, in a grudging, forced, paying-for-the-drink kind of voice.

'No,' I said, nice and casual, but friendly, 'I've only just got back to London. Living it up a bit, you know how it is. I've been doing a stint in the Colonies. Australia, actually.'

It would account, I decided, for all my lapses in current upper-class idiom. Frere grunted, I think in commiseration.

'I thought of Australia once,' he muttered into his glass, as if confessing a sexual lapse to an Irish priest. 'You know, contracting out of the rat-race. What's it like?'

My spirits rose. The sort of person who could talk of going to Australia to contract out of the rat-race was obviously easily fooled.

'Tophole,' I said. 'Sun. Plenty of space. Money.'

A spark of interest crossed his handsome, unlovable face. 'There is money, is there? Still?'

'Oh yes,' I said. 'I had lots of things going for me there. It's easy if you know the right people.'

'Oh, I've got contacts,' said the Honourable Edwin. 'My uncle was Governor of Tasmania, back in the 'fifties some time.'

'Couldn't be better,' I said. 'Australians are pretty impressed by that kind of thing, in spite of what they say. Show 'em a title and they grovel.'

A catlike smile crossed his face, but he volunteered no personal information. 'Tasmania's a pretty nice spot, isn't it?' he said eventually.

'All right. Pretty. Quiet. Sort of like Devon without the buzz of activity. If it's money you're after you wouldn't go there. Sydney's your best bet, if you want to make a pile.'

'I didn't say I was wanting to make money,' Edwin muttered gracelessly.

'You're crazy if you're not, with things as they are these days.'

'True,' he conceded gloomily. 'True enough. Trouble with me isn't not having money. It's getting through it.'

'Don't I know the feeling,' I said. 'I remembered Britain as cheap.'

He remained in contemplation of his glass for a bit, then suddenly put it down on the bar.

'I've got to make a phone call,' he said, and swung off towards a phone in the far corner. Gracious little soul, I thought. I bought myself another drink, calculating that he was more likely to continue talking to me if there was no compulsion on him to buy a round. I looked in his direction. He stood there crouched over the phone, talking urgently; then he gradually relaxed upwards, spread his length against the wall, and began smirking into the mouthpiece. He was a man who was best when he got what he wanted, I thought. At length he put the receiver down and strolled back to the bar, exuding self-love. He glanced at my glass, saw that it was full, and stayed with me.

'My . . . my girl's coming,' he said, oozing a secret smile down into his pale yellow Scotch. My heart leapt up, and it had nothing to do with rainbows in the sky. Surely it couldn't . . . But I had a sneaking feeling that it just could. I wondered whether to beat a hasty retreat.

'Perhaps I'd better have a look at what's going on over there,' I said.

'Nothing going till later,' said Edwin Frere. 'It's just small fry there now. Little people, little winnings. Where do your people come from?'

'Northumberland.'

'Oh yes? Where did you go to school?'

I told him. He was unimpressed. I thought he would turn back to the bar in disgust and drop me till his girl came. But no such luck. He went on effortfully making conversation, asking me what I'd been doing in Australia, where I'd been, who I'd known—there's nothing more depressing, I think, than the 'Did you ever run across old "Chucker" Harbottle' style of conversation. I sank further into fiction, and produced a few imaginary notables of my own for him to deny knowledge of. He kept his end up, in a graceless sort of way, but he kept his eyes skinned around the place, and eventually he was rewarded.

'There she is,' he said, with creamy satisfaction. 'You'll have to meet her.'

And there she was, the Princess Helena herself, dancing gaily into the gaming room, accompanied by the faintly untrustworthy Secretary, and looking for all the world as if she had spent half her life in shady casinos. Silly girl! The trick was to look as if this was a strange and new experience. I looked around me, thinking to make a second bid at retreat, but as she approached the Honourable Edwin gripped me by the arm and brought me upright to be introduced. And that was a laugh, of course, because he had never even asked my name, or told me his.

'But we've met!' said the Princess, wide-eyed and gorgeous. 'Ah, now, it's—'

'Peregrine Tre-mumble, Your Royal Highness,' I managed to mutter, swallowing my all-too-notorious surname.

'Yes, of course. It was at—where was it?'

'A party, Ma'am. I think at Jeremy Styles'.'

It was a name from Joe's dossier, the best-known one, and it was an unlucky choice. Edwin Frere's brow darkened, but the Princess refused to notice.

'That's right. I remember now. There were so *many* there. You're the one who—'

'Just back from Australia, Ma'am,' I cued in. We made a fine romantic duet, we did, a real Ivor Novello and Olive Gilbert. But at least the moment of danger seemed past.

'Ah yes, that's right,' breathed the Princess, hardly at all fazed. 'Oh, I do love Australia! When I was there last year I was never off the front pages. It was the same in the States. People tell me I oughtn't to think about things like that, but I'm sorry to say I do!'

One thing I didn't understand in all this was why the Honourable Edwin had been so keen to keep hold of me, and to introduce me to his prize. Could it be—God forbid!—that he had some suspicion of who I was? If so, we'd put up just about a good enough show to pass muster, I thought. But I changed my mind when I saw the consequence of his introduction. The roulette wheel was now an object of secondary attraction in the room. People started drifting over from the tables and from the card room too, casually collecting around the bar; and some of them were selected by the unlovable Edwin to be introduced to the Princess. Being able, now, to slip to the outskirts of the group, I came to a few conclusions. One was that the principle of selection for this honour was money and power, with money definitely in the lead. The second was that none of these people had been particularly anxious to talk to Edwin Frere before his princess arrived—he had been solitary, perhaps even shunned. I had been used as a signal—that he was willing to introduce people to his prize. Now I could be cast aside, and Edwin could mingle with the favoured, moneyed few. Interesting. I had a feeling that before very long Edwin would be demanding of these chosen few a *quid pro quo*—several quid, in fact. And that they all knew him, had all been touched by him for 'loans' before, and recognized very well the nature of this bargain.

I wondered whether the Princess did too. Because

though she behaved with a sort of feather-brained politeness, she soon disentangled herself from this rather portly and ponderous mob and managed to get herself to my side. It was no great compliment to be found more entertaining than that lot, but in any case the more persistent of them straggled along and introduced themselves to me, bought me drinks (which I accepted) and generally prevented any *tete-à-tete* in which I could perhaps have made clear my opinion of her choice of venue for out-of-hours fun. Not, I suppose, that I would have dared do that anyway. I was beginning to sense the precise geography of that borderland country of behaviour, into which it was dangerous to stray.

So we made conversation—about Australia, about parties, about pop music (concerning which the Princess seemed to have an enormous store of useless information), and the fat industrialists and their fat wives said how they loved the Beatles and wasn't it awful about John Lennon, and quickly changed the subject to Middlesbrough or Derby or wherever they came from so that they could assure the Princess of the great joy her visit to open the local sauna bath for geriatrics had given the populace of these places. Sparkling it was. Frankly, if I had been the young lady I would have given the swift boot to any boy-friend who involved me in tedious encounters of this kind—especially one who then left me in the lurch and patently pursued ends of his own, as Edwin Frere was at that moment doing. In fact, I did at one stage think I caught the shadow of a distinctly royal displeasure cross her face when she looked in his direction. Mostly however, training held, and she maintained an air of composure and vague goodwill.

What was not to be doubted, though, was her pleasure when she caught sight of a new arrival.

'Jeremy!' she said, to a figure lounging in through the main door. 'What a lovely surprise!'

As a surprise I rated it a good deal lower. I kicked myself again for mentioning the name of Jeremy Styles when I could have come up with any old fictitious one. But Styles was an actor, and who could have expected him to show up here? Luckily the Princess appreciated the problem, dragged me over to him crying 'Peregrine you know, don't you?', and then took us both off to the safety of the bar.

Danger over, I thought. But I wasn't too happy when Styles told the barman to line up three doubles, just for him.

Styles, as I said, was in a new play at the St George's. Unluckily it was one of those two- or three-character jobs which is all anyone can afford to put on in the West End these days, and consequently it ended rather early, when the duologue ran thin. He was a bit greasepainty behind the ears, and generally had the look of still being half on stage. He was, of course, immensely handsome, even—I have to admit it—magnetic. His whole body had a tense energy which demanded to be noticed, and he made himself felt and understood even over a wide radius. Some of the Birmingham drearies, for example, showed signs of wanting to join us, but it needed no more than a pregnant stare to make them swerve aside to the other end of the bar. He had fair, cornlike hair, wavy and clinging round his shirt collar at the back; he had arrogant eyes, delicately hooked nose, and an egotistical mouth, the sort that announces that its owner is not to be crossed. But you've probably seen him on television scores of times: he's played Stephen Guest and Mr Darcy on the screen, and George Osborne in a stage musical of *Vanity Fair*. He looks good in breeches, and knows how to sit down in a swallow-tail coat. But I have to admit he looked all right whatever he wore, and the Princess obviously thought so too.

'Jeremy is an actor,' she announced happily. 'I'm sure

you've seen him on television.'

'Many times,' I said. 'I enjoyed your Mr Darcy very much.'

'Oh, it got to Australia, did it?' said the Princess wickedly.

Styles had nodded off-handedly at my compliment, and now he said: 'Some private joke?'

'Very,' said the Princess Helena. 'How did the performance go tonight?'

'Quite well,' said Styles. 'Very well, really. We haven't had time to go stale. The audience is still lively. The American summer invasion hasn't got under way.'

'Do you prefer the stage to television?' I asked.

'Of course he does,' said Helena. 'It's in his blood.'

Jeremy Styles scowled: 'I prefer television,' he muttered.

'I didn't realize you came of an acting family,' I said.

'Oh God,' said Jeremy Styles.

'He does,' said the Princess, 'but he doesn't talk about them, except when he's drunk, do you, darling?'

As if to illustrate her point, Styles downed his second whisky and began talking about them, gesturing all the time with a sort of erratic theatricality.

'You wouldn't have heard of them. My mother was a sort of second-string leading lady. Used to take over leading roles after the plays had run a year or so. Or take over for the tours, in the days when we still had provincial touring theatres. She was a bitch, an arrant, rampant, straight-down-the-line bitch. She dragged along my father when it was possible—he took small roles, and they brought in enough to cover the cost of his brandy. People ten rows back used to send notes of complaint to the theatre management. When there was no part for him, or when the directors were fed up with his slurred incompetence, she latched on to someone else for the duration. I was dumped in the dressing-room, dumped in the theatre bedroom, even locked in the wardrobe one whole night, when I cried. That was my childhood.'

'You're just making a good moan out of it,' said Helena. 'It must have been awfully exciting, really.'

'You think so? Do you know, I could barely read when I was nine. The thing was so notorious that someone informed the local educational authority of some dreary burgh where we happened to be camped for some period longer than a week. My parents pulled the charming gypsies act—they were bringing me up as a child of nature. But the rest of the company didn't play up. They had to send me to school—dumped into a tiny private school in a dumpy town in Essex, chosen because it was cheap and difficult to get to on visits. I'd seen so few kids I didn't know what playing meant.'

'Doesn't sound much worse than being royal,' said the Princess.

'I wonder you went on stage yourself,' I said, trying to puncture the self-pity. Jeremy Styles shrugged his expressive shoulders.

'I was seduced by a theatrical knight at the age of fifteen. He got me a job carrying spears in *Julius Cæsar*, and shoved himself up me regularly between dying in battle and being pronounced the noblest Roman of them all. Since then I've never been out of a job. It's not as though work is easy to come by these days. Besides, I'm not fit for anything else.'

'Doomed,' said the Princess. Jeremy Styles looked at her petulantly, as if used to being taken seriously.

A shadow passed over the table. I looked up. It was Edwin Frere—fair and flushed, with a mixture of uncertainty and ill-temper in his face.

'Oh Helena,' he said. 'I want you to come and meet a friend of mine.'

The way he put it was hardly respectful, and the Princess reacted.

'Not now, Edwin,' she said coolly, and turned back to us. Jeremy Styles, who had just downed his third whisky, was by now looking as flushed as Frere. He sniggered insultingly.

'You're with me, remember, Helena,' said Frere, compounding his sin.

'I'm not, so far as I know, with anyone,' said Helena. 'I came on my own. Leave us alone for a bit, will you, Edwin?'

Jeremy Styles extended himself elegantly in his chair, and drawled: 'Yes, go back to playing "touch", can't you, Frere?'

People for miles around could see that an insult had been intended, and an instant hush descended over the bar.

'What the hell did you say?' demanded Frere, stepping closer, but with bluster in his tone.

'You heard. Leave us alone.'

'You goddamned little player, you—'

Styles got to his feet.

'Get out of my light, Frere. Don't start acting as if you'd got rights. There are other claims staked here.'

I had got to my feet, and I took them both by the collars and dragged them apart.

'For God's sake act your age,' I told Styles. 'You're not fourteen.'

'All actors are fourteen,' hissed Styles. 'Just get that upper-class sponge off our backs, will you, and—'

But I wasn't listening to him. I suddenly realized that the Princess Helena was no longer at the table, and was heading unobtrusively for the door. I dived out after her, and caught her up at the top of the stairs. As we darted down them, I heard the sound of a table overturning behind us.

'Right,' said Helena briskly. 'The car is just down the road. Signal it, and I'll be with you by the time it gets here.'

And she briskly dispensed with the fawnings and toadyings of the casino manager at the foot of the stairs, sending him up to the sounds of unarmed combat above. She threw her coat elegantly over her shoulders, and glided through the main entrance and down to the car, where I stood holding the door open for her.

'Get in with me,' she said, and we started off.

Once speeding towards the Palace, she relaxed.

'*Weren't* they naughty,' she giggled, with childish pleasure. '*Just* the sort of scene I absolutely oughtn't to be involved in.'

'I should think not, Ma'am,' I said. 'You got out of it very smoothly.'

'I did, didn't I? But it's happened before.'

Really the coolness of the lady frightened me.

'Wouldn't it be better to be a bit careful about going to places like that?' I said. 'Ma'am.'

She looked at me, wide-eyed and giggling.

'But I wouldn't have missed it for the world!' she said. 'Frightfully exciting!'

I was reminded of an Ibsen heroine: wasn't it Hilde Wangel who went around saying things like that? But another name occurred to me still more forcefully: Hedda Gabler, the lady who liked to make exciting things happen around her. The very thought made the blood run cold. I was responsible for the security of a royal Hedda Gabler.

CHAPTER 5

House Visiting

The phone call came next morning while I was shaving, and while Jan was somewhat blearily giving Daniel his breakfast cornflakes (for she had been busy way into the night pumping me for details of the previous night's fracas, with all the persistent gentleness of a KGB inquisitor). I wiped myself free of lather and went out into the little hall, knowing somehow I wasn't going to like it.

'Perry Trethowan,' I said.

'I know,' said the voice at the other end. 'Big Perry of Scotland Yard, no less, whose father was done in while doing his evening bend-and-stretch.'

'Who *is* that?' I said frostily (because that is a topic I always nip in the bud).

'Don't you recognize the voice? The voice you heard playing Mr Darcy on television—the series you saw while you were down under?'

'Oh,' I said.

'I just wanted to tell you I'd blown your cover—is that the expression? I never get roles in spy stories; not seedy enough, I suppose. I puzzled and puzzled over who you were through my drunken haze last night—after I'd blacked that little pimp's eye and been politely shown the door. This morning it came to me in a flash. Actors always say there's no such thing as bad publicity, but I suppose the same doesn't go for policemen, does it?'

'There's no question of blowing my cover,' I muttered untruthfully. 'I'm in charge of the Princess's security.'

'Then why all that garbage about Australia? But don't worry, I won't gab. I like the thought of your keeping an eye on that upper-class ponce—even if you are keeping it on me at the same time.'

'Hmmm,' I said, making my uncertainty rather obvious. 'Would you mind if I came round to see you some time?'

'Any time. Come round to my dressing-room before the show. Or I'm in the book, under my real name.'

'What's your real name?'

'Mervyn Bowles. We all have our guilty secrets, don't we?'

Well, I suppose I should have expected it. It will be a few years before I can attain anonymity again. In the circumstances it seemed sensible to attempt no more cover-ups of who I was, or of what I was doing, though there was every reason not to broadcast the special fears we had for the Princess's safety. Although it was certainly not normal practice to case the friends and boy-friends of royal personages (except, of course, very discreetly, if they were in any way contentious), the current crop were not to know this. I intended one way or another to interview them all. But that wasn't the only thing on my plate, or even the most immediate. I had to go over all the routines of royal protection, and as soon as possible I intended taking a trip to Knightley. The death of Bill Tredgold interested me, and I wasn't sure that the police had done as much as they might in that direction.

So that morning I accompanied the Princess on a visit to a canning factory in East London. There seemed no particular reason for the visit, except perhaps to support those few areas of British industry not actually bankrupt, and it was all stupendously boring, I can tell you. All there is to report is that the Princess behaved admirably throughout: she almost convinced even me that she was interested in what she was shown. And the lady-in-waiting—whose name, I gathered, was Lady Dorothy Lowndes-Gore—kept close, maintained a profile lower than a snake's armpit, and drawled out odd little driblets of conversation with the firm's functionary deputed to look after her. So we all did our job, but really it was a right drag, and after a dreary lunch I was happy to be able to deliver them back to the side entrance of Kensington Palace and follow my own devices.

My own devices took me to a very different palace.

I knew the Palace of Westminster better than I had known Kensington Palace. I had had a stint of guarding the assembled Lords and Commons during my early days in the Force. It had mostly consisted of standing at the main entrance looking impressive, and answering questions of stupendous idiocy ('Where is Margaret Thatcher's powder room?' or 'Is this St Paul's Cathedral?') from every nation, colour and creed under the sun. Not an enlivening period of my life. Still, I knew the place, the routines, even some of the personnel. It seemed a good idea to beard Harry Bayle there, rather than at home. Perhaps even observe him in action. So I made my way to the Mother of Parliaments.

The people in charge of security and handling the public at Westminster are a stable lot. Me, I'd regard it as a life sentence in a madhouse, but some of them seem quite to like it: it adds a new dimension to the television news. Anyway, knowing some of them from my earlier stint helped a lot, because things were a bit hectic there, in preparation for a big debate on Trade Union reform, due to start later in the afternoon. It was like a bank holiday football match. The place was swarming with seedy Union officials backed up by real horny-handed sons of toil, all of them going through the charade of pretending that anything anyone did could persuade the Prime Minister to change her mind. Such pretences are part of the democratic process, I suppose, but they are also powerful aphrodisiacs to inflated egos. Everyone was huffing and puffing like mad. I got one of the boys aside and told him what I wanted.

'Harry Bayle?' said Sergeant Crosse, gentle, firm and unflappable. 'Well, I know he's meeting the boilermakers at half past three, and then the sheet-metal people at five. And he's bound to want to talk in the debate, if he can catch the Speaker's eye. He pisses the Speaker off, by the by, so he leans over backwards to be fair to him. He may even have a question down . . .' He consulted the order paper. 'Yes, he does. Would you like to see him in action?'

I would indeed. So Crosse led me through various

passages, full of members of the public with special passes from their MPs, and finally I found myself in the well-remembered shadow at the back of the public gallery. It was full, in anticipation of the debate, and so was the House. MPs, like actors, give of their best to a full house, and lots of them try to get in on the act if they know they have constituents in the gallery, to prove they're alive. I gazed down on the opposition benches, full of Libs and Labs and Social Democrats; and there, sitting with studied ease but really panting to be heard, was Harry Bayle.

He'd been Henry in his first election addresses, of course, but since then his matiness had grown with his arrogance. His father had been a bank manager—and one has to be wary of the matiness of bank managers too. Henry had been brought up in a highly genteel Hertfordshire town, gone to a minor public school, seemed destined for a life of middle-class comfort somewhere in the gin-and-tonic belt. But then at Oxford he had swerved to the left, professing all sorts of nonsenses traceable back to Cultural Revolution slogans. He'd righted himself as soon as he got his degree, and he'd got himself elected in 1974 as a sort of Wilsonian Socialist, if that isn't a totally meaningless description. He was then twenty-four—not the baby of the house, but definitely kindergarten. He hadn't behaved with the modesty and deference appropriate to his youth and newness. He had veered rapidly left again, attached himself to Tony Benn, but then, after a disagreement with that gentleman's acolytes, had more recently begun staking out a left-wing pasture of his own. Jan's parents, whenever they saw him on television, muttered, 'He gets his orders from Moscow'—they are working-class Tories of the worst kind, and their vocabulary of abuse is hardly of today, when the line-up in Red Square looks like a day outing from a particularly dreary old people's home. I couldn't see Harry Bayle taking orders from them. I think he had an instinct for the main chance and took orders from it.

And here he was, on his feet now; tall, striking-looking, with dark straight hair deliberately not too tidy; he exuded confidence, and had a ringing voice that had had its middle-class, home counties twang flattened out into classlessness.

'Is the Minister aware—?' Oh God, is the Minister aware. How I hate their jargon! The assumption that the Minister ought to sit up all night pondering the defective sewage system of Much-Piddlebury-on-the-Wold. It's just another aspect of their appalling self-importance, and it really got me down when I had to listen to it every day. Actually, in this case the matter of which the Minister ought to be aware was a thoroughly disgraceful case of a firm which employed immigrant women, grossly underpaying them, and resisting any attempts they made to unionize themselves. One would have been totally on Harry Bayle's side if one hadn't had the suspicion that the question was designed to improve his ratings with the anti-racial, feminist and Trade Union lobbies, and that it had been put down for today in anticipation of his meetings later with the boilermakers and the sheet-metal workers. In the public gallery I noticed grizzled heads nodding approval.

Anyway, the question and supplementaries, and the answers from the Junior Minister (all about giving time for the due processes, not rushing in, the determination of the government not to intervene in matters which—you know the patter: business as usual at Westminster) took about five minutes, and at the end Harry Bayle sat down, obviously well satisfied. After sitting through the next question or two, for form's sake, he slipped out of the chamber. And so did I.

By the time I got back to the main hall, he was there himself. He was clutching a batch of papers and an attaché case, and seemed to be on his way somewhere, but he had got tangled with some constituents, and he was glad-handing them in a big way. It was 'Bill' this and 'Sally' that, and clapping Jim on the back and putting his arm around Betty, and lots of laughter and ribbing. Watching him from a distance I could see he was itching to get off in search of stray Trade Unionists around the place: it was, after all, Trade Unionists who had the big say in Labour Party elections these days. But he didn't let them see this, not at all, because he managed the whole encounter very nicely indeed. I began to see that there was more to him than the smart political operator: there was the power-seeker, the crowd-pleaser, the publicity manipulator and the pure and simple shit.

It was as he was extricating himself from the devoted tentacles of Bill and Sally and Jim and Betty that I approached him.

'Mr Bayle? I'm Superintendent Trethowan, CID. I wonder if I could have a word with you for a moment? Just a little matter of security.'

He was obviously annoyed at being interrupted in his purposes again, and he put on a rather sickening smile.

'Security? Really, is it necessary? I don't think any of my constituents wants to assassinate me.'

He was gesturing towards them in a sycophantic way when I said: 'It was the security of the Princess Helena that I wanted to talk about, sir.'

He froze. He looked like an Archbishop of Canterbury who has just been accused of owning half shares in a pædophiliac brothel. After a full second, and a swallow, he shook himself and ushered me over to a corner.

'*Really*,' he said, settling himself down on to a bench with his bag and papers. 'Did you have to do that?'

'I'm sorry. Did I say something wrong?'

'Well, you might have realized that . . .' He found it impossible, or too embarrassing, to explain. 'Oh, never mind. I suppose one can't expect too much sensitivity from the fuzz.'

'Quite,' I said. 'We're not paid for our quivering sensibility. I take it that you mean your constituents would be shocked by your associating with the royal family?'

'Most of them would be tickled pink. But those particular ones . . . Well, I might not be able to convince them that to me she's just—just a—'

'Yes?'

'Oh, get on with it, man. What is this all about?'

I launched myself confidently into the sea of untruth.

'The fact is, sir, we've reason to believe that there may be a threat to the Princess's life—in fact, from the IRA.' (Thank God for the IRA! What would we do without it? Have to go back to the old-fashioned anarchists, I suppose.) 'This being the case, we're naturally checking up on all the Princess's . . . contacts, so I should want to talk to you in any case, since we gather you've been seeing something of each other. What worries us about you, sir, is that *together* you would make such a doubly inviting target.'

I obviously wasn't convincing him. His face slid into a sneer of disbelief.

'Oh, come on, now, Inspector, or whatever you are. I'm pretty well known to be on the left of the party. I've no particular interest in Ireland, but it's us those boys get on best with. We speak up for them from time to time. It's the Conservatives these chaps would want to get at, particularly now they're in power.'

'Unfortunately,' I said, 'the Princess is not associating with any Conservatives at the moment. She is associating with you. And as far as we can see, you could be a brace of sitting birds.'

He sat there, complacent, impatient, not open to conviction. 'This sounds like a lot of police bullshit to me, if you don't mind my saying so. I've always said that the police create more crime than they solve.'

'It's a point of view,' I said, suave, very suave. 'I've heard people say that politicians create more problems than they solve. We all have our critics. Tell me, sir, where have you and the Princess been accustomed to meet?'

'Oh, we met at a film première. Charity do. I don't hold much with charities – most of them are just excuses for bourgeois do-gooding – but I do sit on a Parliamentary Commission on the British film industry. I think we're meant to find out if it still exists. That's why I was there.'

'I see. But that wasn't quite my question. I asked you where you had been accustomed to meet.'

He floundered visibly. 'Well . . . we've met at parties, that kind of thing . . . been to the theatre, though frankly that's a bit too public for me . . . met in my flat.'

'Ah yes, that would be at – ?'

'I live in Dolphin Square.'

'Yes, I know that. But according to our information the flat you took the Princess to was in – '

'So you've been following us?' He flung open his arms in an angry gesture. 'I've half a mind to ask a question of the Home Secretary about that.'

'I doubt whether, on thinking it over, you will want to, sir.'

He was not dim. That thought had struck him even as he said it. He gave in with bad grace.

'Oh, all right then. The fact is, some of us here have a place – a sort of *pied-à-terre* – where we can go to, to – you know. My wife lives in the constituency, but she's taken to coming up to London unexpectedly. She caught me once, and – well, I don't have to spell it out to you, I suppose. So there's this little flat down river – it used to be Price-Feverel's, before he married – and we club together to pay the rent, and . . .'

Well, well, I thought. Price-Feverel was a Conservative, a Junior Treasury Minister, one of the rigid monetarist types the PM seemed to get on best with. An inter-party knocking shop, then! Well, well, as I said. Good to see that some things transcend party barriers.

'There's really no cause for embarrassment, sir,' I said, reapplying the suavity. 'That sort of thing is no concern of mine, so long as you keep within the law. It's only a question of knowing where the Princess might be if she is with you. Of course, one would like to be sure that the IRA knows nothing about this flat.'

'Oh, come on, Inspector, you don't really think they trail us when we slip out for a quick naughty, do you?'

'That is exactly what I do think, sir. They might very well enjoy catching you with, so to speak, your trousers down. They are probably not without a sense of humour.'

'I'd say that is exactly what they are without, and I'm sure I know them better than you, Inspector. I had something to do with them while I was at Oxford.'

Of course. He was in student politics at the time when young left-wingers would express solidarity with anyone provided they threw bombs. But I refrained from following him up the garden path after my own red herring. I did not think the IRA had anything to do with this.

'What I came to ask you, sir, was this,' I said. 'You can see that if there is a threat of any kind to the Princess, it presents the police with special problems.'

'I'm not really very interested in the police's problems.'

'But perhaps you might be a mite interested in the young lady's safety?' He pursed his lips. It wasn't quite on to say he didn't give a bugger. 'It's particularly difficult because we're anxious not to let the Princess know we're especially worried. What I'd like you to do is this: if you're going out with the Princess, could you phone this number and leave a message telling me where you both are? Just "Bayle, 35 Cheyne Walk", that kind of thing.'

I handed him a card with a Scotland Yard number on it, but he took it only with reluctance, and stuffed it in with his papers.

'Really, I don't know . . . This does seem like an intolerable invasion of privacy.'

'Even though the Princess's life may be at stake?' I asked. And as he seemed so little concerned, I added: 'And yours too.'

'Oh, very well.' He looked at his watch, scowled, and began stuffing his papers into his briefcase. 'You've made me late for the boilermakers. But I'll co-operate as far as I can.'

A paper fluttered to the floor and I picked it up for him. It was an old election address. It had a picture of Harry Bayle, his wife, and two little boys. The wife was sensible-looking rather than glamorous—a down-to-earth, busy, right-thinking body, a typical Labour Party wife.

'Nice picture,' I said, handing it back to him.

CHAPTER 6

Country Pleasures

I'd got the idea that the next day was to hold another factory visit for the Princess. When I had started on the case I had gone through the Court Circulars and 'Social Engagements' columns of the papers, constructing the Princess's round of activities for the last few and the next few months. But there must have been a change of plan, because when I rang Joplin that evening I found that next day was to be the first of two days of engagements in the

Midlands. The opportunity was too good to be missed. I told Joplin that both of us would be going with her, but that I would be sloping off for a time to Knightley. I had a date with the dead Bill Tredgold.

Well, we took the Royal train up to Birmingham—attended to the platform at Euston Station by all manner of station-masters and things, top-hatted and togged up to the nines, and all the more conspicuous when compared to the slovenliness and grime of all the other functionaries in sight. All the bowing and scraping was enough to make a cat laugh, but the Princess took it all in her stride—her demeanour commonsensical (didn't everyone who went by train get this sort of treatment?) and a shade demure. I sat on the train with her and Lady Muck, in what was not so much a compartment as a large, rather plush room. Joplin patrolled the corridors, and seemed to consider himself well out of it. The Princess Helena and I talked about the day's engagements, read the papers, commented on the news. The Princess read the *Daily Grub* for preference, which rather shocked me. In spite of that, though, I was beginning to revise my opinion about her intelligence. She might not have an idea in her head, not an idea of the abstract kind, but she did have a useful practical streak, a knowledge of where to draw the line, an ability to deal with people, and get them to do what she wanted. She coped admirably, for example, with Lady Dorothy Lowndes-Gore. She sat, upright and cool, in the corner of the apartment on wheels, reading one of those glossies that assumes its readers run a couple of Rolls and have more Georgian silver than they know what to do with. The Princess, in the midst of our chat, kept throwing remarks in her direction, and paid solemn attention to her drawled, inhibited replies. I could see she wished her a hundred miles away, so we could have a cosy chat about the fracas in the Wellington Club, but not by a whisker did she give any sign of this.

The only time Lady Dorothy made any independent remark, it was addressed to me: 'You're one of the Northumberland Trethowans, aren't you?'

'I was,' I said.

She looked at me for a moment, as if my answer smacked of Jacobinism. Then she said: 'I met your cousin Peter once,' and dropped her head down once more into her glossy. I rather got the impression that much of her conversation was of this kind, that she acted as a Waugh-like ancestral voice, charting the ramifications of the Great Families, and lamenting their downfall.

The engagement for the morning was of the Princess Helena's traditional type: we all visited an old people's home that was celebrating its fiftieth anniversary. You can imagine what it was like: product of the Depression, its aim was obviously to produce just that in anybody who had anything to do with it today. There was a smell of new paint, obviously for the visit, but through doors one caught glimpses of peeling walls, sagging ceilings and arthritic sofas in the rooms the Princess was not to be taken into. The staff seemed to be recruited from the female relatives of Methodist missionaries, and the old people themselves gave every appearance of waiting impatiently for the last feeble spark to be extinguished.

In this sort of environment the Princess flowered, like an outrageous orchid in a herbaceous border. She smiled, she flashed those splendid eyes, she bent solicitously over and chatted, and she made the staff feel they were a cross between Florence Nightingale and Elizabeth Fry, fit only for translation to a heavenly home, or for CBEs at the very least. I began to appreciate her, not as a person, but as a *performer*: on duty she was a non-stop, never-flag *show*. At length we all tottered into the dining-room for drinks and lunch. The old people, we gathered, would be partaking of a 'light lunch' (cabbage-stalks and potato peelings, most probably) elsewhere in the building.

The array of local worthies we were lumbered with was a mixed bunch. There were lots of the sort of red-faced, paunchy businessmen we'd met at the Wellington, whose rubicund, heavy-lidded aspect told of business lunches, and wage negotiations into the early hours. Then there were the Midlands gentry, consciously giving the event tone. They self-consciously left the Princess to the commercial interest—rather implying that *they* could talk to her any day of the week. I was given a drink to hold (I suspect on the direction of the lady-in-waiting, who had decided that I could not be treated like any old policeman), and I tried to mingle while not letting my guard down. I found myself talking—my eye on the Princess all the time—to someone who seemed to be a nob of some kind.

The conversation turned out to be an elegant variation on the lady-in-waiting's family obsession: we played the 'I suppose you know' game.

'I hear you're one of the Northumberland Trethowans. Everyone survive that nasty business last year?'

'Everyone except my father,' I said. 'Mostly they thrived on it.'

'Harpenden's close to the Yorkshire border, isn't it? I suppose you know the Witteringhams?'

'I think I may have—'

'And the Northumberland Fortescues. Not the Derbyshire lot, but the younger branch. Now, they wouldn't be all that far from you, would they?'

'No, about twenty—'

'I say,' he interrupted, with a sort of nervous intensity that covered the rudeness, 'wasn't your mother one of the Cumberland Godriches? You know, I think we must be related. I say, Dot—wasn't my Aunt Margaret second cousin or something to the Cumberland Godriches?'

'Yes, through her maternal grandmother,' drawled Lady Dorothy.

I was surprised to hear Lady Dorothy addressed as Dot, but not surprised to hear she had everyone's family tree at the tips of her well-manicured fingers. The conversation pissed me off no end, but after a bit I got him on to horses and dogs, which I suspected were the only other things he knew anything about, and eventually we sat down to lunch. Lunch was one of those predictable disasters which occur when cooking staff used to making boiled fish and cottage pie try to do something a little special. After it, farewells were said, little speeches made, and the Princess was driven off to the home of the Lord Lieutenant of the County, where she was staying overnight. Later in the day she was to attend Beckett at the Birmingham Rep, but seniority goes for nothing if you can't hand that sort of job over to the lower ranks, so I delivered the Princess, like a gorgeous parcel, into the safe-keeping of Joplin, commandeered a car from the Birmingham CID (who had been informed of my mission and had promised all co-operation) and about four o'clock hit the road for Knightley.

Knightley, it turned out, was a charming little village of about four or five hundred inhabitants: not one of the Shropshire showplaces, not an obvious venue for Housman fanciers bent on tracing the course of the celebrated Lad from plough-shaft to gallows, but still a very pleasant little place indeed. I could see no obvious reason why Bill Tredgold should have found himself here, unless the reason was the hotel itself, where he spent his last night. It doubled as the local pub, called itself The Wrekin, and was a splendid Elizabethan half-timber job with about thirty-odd bedrooms, which no doubt filled up nicely in the summer and in the spring holiday periods. It was not one of those places that aim to provide every mod. con. to go with the frisson of uneven floors and oak-beamed ceilings. In fact, I doubted whether much modernization had taken place in the last fifty years or so. But it was comfortable and unpretentious, while being just that bit run down as well. Even the foyer, where the hotel reception was, had a nicely lived-in appearance, as if generations of farmers had eased their ample bottoms down into the armchairs.

It was the owner who came when I rang, and I booked in for the night. I liked the look of the man, so I opened in on the subject immediately.

'I'm afraid you're not going to like this, but in point of fact, I'm Police. Scotland Yard. It's that business of William Tredgold again.'

'Good God, surely we've had enough of you here going into that, haven't we? It's not good for business, you know.'

'It might be better for business to have had a murder in the place than to have had a leaky gas-fire,' I pointed out.

'Perhaps,' the owner admitted gloomily. 'That's not the sort of publicity we like though, either way. Look, you'd better come through to the office.'

So I went round the desk and settled snugly into the little den behind—more of the threadbare old furniture, and a nice coal fire for both of us to sit around. He introduced himself as Terence Shaply: he was about fifty-five—a capable, intelligent chap, the sort who might have retired here from his own business, enjoying both the occasional bustle and the normal humdrum course of things. I had no doubt the place was well-run, in an unostentatious sort of way.

I said: 'Look, I have the details of the previous investigations, but it might be helpful if you went over the main points again.'

He sighed. 'That's what they all say. Well, here goes. He—or rather they—checked in somewhere around seven o'clock.'

'Had the room been reserved in advance?'

'Oh yes, earlier in the day. I took the call myself.'

'So it definitely wasn't just a casual visit—they hadn't just been driving through and decided to stop.'

'Oh no, we get quite a bit of that sort of custom, but this wasn't one of that kind. To tell you the truth, they didn't seem to know each other that well, and I'm afraid I assumed it was a dirty weekend, arranged pretty much on the spur.'

'You hadn't had him before, for that reason?'

'Never seen him in my life, to my knowledge.'

'Do you—don't be offended—do you get many people here on dirty weekends? You're not, so to speak, known for it?'

'Certainly not! Many more likely places than us for that. If we have dirty weekenders it's likely to be the quiet here that attracts them. In other words, one or both of them are probably married.'

'Yes—and that wasn't the case here.'

'No, I gather not. Well, he booked in at the desk there, and we swapped a few remarks about the weather. She stood well aside, and didn't say anything. They went up to their room, weren't up there long, and then came down and had dinner. That's when I got the idea they didn't know each other all that well—'

'Why?'

'Well, the conversation was just that bit forced: lots of jokes and laughing, but some awkward silences too. They played footy under the table, and giggled. You don't do that if you've been going out with each other any length of time.'

'Indeed not. What did they do next?'

'They didn't linger over dinner. They went straight upstairs, and that was the last anyone here saw of them. Alive.'

'I see. I suppose in the morning one of the maids smelt the gas, did she?'

'That's right.'

'There are two interesting points here, aren't there? First of all the gas-fire.'

'Right. We're still on the sort of gas-fire that was installed twenty or thirty years ago—these were put in before my time, but are still quite serviceable. We've had this one inspected, naturally, and the police had a look at it too, and they say there was no fault there, and no reason why the flame should have gone out. Of course, most people would turn it off before they went to sleep.'

'Perhaps they did,' I said. 'Perhaps they did. Now the other thing is the wine, isn't it?'

'Yes. I must say I find that odd. There were glasses, you see, two glasses. And they certainly weren't the hotel's glasses. Of course they could have brought them with them, but they had very little luggage, and it seems an odd thing to pack. Most people who bring a bottle of anything to drink in their rooms use the bathroom glasses. And then, you see, it was white wine—so if they brought it with them they must have drunk it unchilled. Perfectly possible, but most people would have brought red.'

'Had they drunk wine at dinner?'

'Yes. A bottle of white—a Jugoslav Riesling.'

'Did they have a corkscrew with them?'

'No, they didn't. Apparently they'd brought glasses, but not a corkscrew. That was one of the things that worried the police here, right from the beginning. On the other hand, you can get your bottle opened for you in the shop where you buy it.'

'Certainly. There's an awful lot of *slightly* odd things that *could* be explained. If they *had* ordered wine up to their room, who would have taken it up to them?'

'Anyone might. Whoever happened to be free in the dining-room or the bar. Or it might be myself or my wife. This isn't the sort of place where you have uniformed maids or wine-waiters.'

'Could I see the hotel register for that day?'

'Surely. Just that day? Several of the guests that night would have been here some days already.'

'I'm assuming that the person I'm interested in would have decided to come here only when Tredgold and his girl came. But you're quite right, it could conceivably be more in the nature of an accidental meeting here. In fact, I'd like a list of everyone in the hotel that night, if you can rustle one up.'

The register showed five married couples to have booked in on the same day as Tredgold, and also three men and two women in singles. I noted them all down, and their place of origin, mentally registering more interest in the people in single rooms: murderers rarely hunt in pairs. When Terence Shaply had rustled up the complete guest list we went back into the foyer. He said: 'Like to have the room they had?'

'Yes,' I said, and he gave me the key to Room 39.

The Wrekin ran true to form for its kind: corridors that rose and fell like the North Sea, odd side passages leading to laundry cupboards, steps with no rational excuse for being there. No. 39 was near the end of a passage, and I have to admit that when I opened the door I got the silliest eerie feeling. I tried to suppress this access of schoolgirlishness: after all, probably every room in the house had had someone die in it at one time or another. Still, this was so recent, and so subtly nasty. But when I got in and looked around, the feeling left me: this was just another hotel room—more irregular than some, but not as large as you sometimes get in these old places. The window had a wonderful view out on to the Shropshire hills. I put my bag on the bed and sat down on a rather insubstantial upright chair. As far as the room itself was concerned, there was nothing now to be done that hadn't already been done. I had no fatuous idea of finding a vital scrap of material which had caught on a nail, or suchlike detective-story clues. With current standards of service in hotels any such clue could have been left by any guest over the past two or three years. On the other hand, this did seem to be the ideal place to think the thing through—if, indeed, *thing* there was.

Ignoring for the moment the possibility of accident, how could the murder have been done? They had drunk white wine at dinner—and could have been seen to do so by any other guest, or of course by the hotel staff. They then came up to this room, with obvious intentions. Assuming this murder wasn't well premeditated (and in detail it could not be, granted that Tredgold had only booked into the hotel that evening), the murderer then had to make his plans. First he had to get hold of a bottle of white wine. Where from? If he was a guest he could order it from room service, but surely that was too risky. From a pub, then, or from Shrewsbury, which was only twelve miles away. Both options involved a car, but I imagined most—perhaps all—the night's guests at the hotel came by car.

So he picked up the wine, and presumably the glasses, at a late-night wine merchant's or from a pub (a Shrewsbury pub would be safest, and least likely to remember a customer who bought a bottle of wine, and conceivably pinched a couple of their glasses). But what then? How to get them to accept and drink it?

Perhaps one should not make too much of that. Britain has become so dizzyingly alcoholic in the last couple of decades that few people will look a gift bottle in the neck. Posing as one of the hotel servants (no need to dress up for that, because as the owner had implied it wasn't that kind of hotel), the murderer could knock on the door, pretend that the hotel was celebrating something (the owner's silver wedding, or the building's four hundredth anniversary, perhaps) and explain that all the guests were getting drinks on the house in celebration, 'And as you had been drinking white wine at dinner, the owner thought . . .' Thin, but probably adequate. With one proviso: for this work, the murderer could not conceivably be known to Bill Tredgold.

And the wine, of course, was drugged. The drug could very easily have been brought with the murderer, in case of opportunity. And when they fell asleep, tired but happy, the murderer could sneak in, in the middle of the night, and turn on the gas-fire. The bedroom door was a rickety Yale lock, presenting no problem to anyone with a bank card. Very neat, very simple, and after this time all but impossible to prove. There was no reason why the murderer should have left any trace of himself behind him, and in the morning he could be up early and away before the deaths were even discovered. If murder there had been, it looked like a hopeless case, from the police point of view.

Nevertheless, some lines of future enquiry did suggest themselves. I took out my notebooks, which so far were practically virgin as far as useful leads on the case were concerned, and after some thought, wrote:

'Why here?'

Why come away for a weekend with your bird, when you've got a perfectly good flat of your own to go to? One answer to that would be that Bill or his girl just felt like a weekend away. Still, there could be other answers. Journalists are very good at mixing business and pleasure (frequently to the detriment of the former), and choosing this place, which apparently neither of them had been to before, did suggest that the excursion had more than one end in view. This put me on to another line of thought. I wrote again: 'What about his luggage?' and 'Reporter's notebook.'

One thing was certain: he would not have travelled, even on a purely pleasure trip, without a notebook of some kind. Reporters never did. Who had it now? His parents?

All this was vague, but to me necessary, because various new lines of enquiry were opening up, as far as I could see. Hitherto we had seen the most likely explanation for Tredgold's death as being that it was an attempt on the life of the Princess. On the other hand, if the murderer, coming in with the wine, had seen the girl (if, in other words, she did not conceal herself under the bedclothes with shame, which was hardly likely in this day and age), then he would certainly have known she was not the Princess. But the murder could still have succeeded rather than failed: the intended victim could have been Bill Tredgold or Carol Crossley, his bird. And if it was Bill, there was no reason totally to rule out the possibility that the Princess was still involved. He had recently been sleeping with her, and his reporter's instinct (a nice way of saying his nose for dirt) could have smelt something fishy going on around her. In which case, it was a fair bet that the details would be in his notebook.

The rest of the day was spent pleasantly, but not very productively. I questioned the staff and the owner's wife about the procedures when wine was ordered to a room, trying to discover whether any of the other guests had ordered wine that day, but I was not surprised when I drew a blank. I phoned the Shrewsbury police, with whom my coming had been cleared in advance, and had them start an enquiry for anyone who had bought a bottle of white wine in a public house, and perhaps in some way got hold of glasses at the same time. I told them also to check the wine dealers, but asking about people who had bought a bottle of wine there three months before really did seem to be wasting the Salop police's time most unconscionably. Then I went and sat with the locals in the public bar, drawing, once again, very much a blank. Not, of course, that they were not interested in the matter: the death of these two—'not wed, they weren't, an' too much on their minds to worry about a little bit of gas,' etc., etc.—would in any case have been the local event of the year. If it were to turn out to be murder, it would be the event of the century. Whisper had already got around about this possibility, but it didn't prevent the locals finding the whole thing rib-nudgingly funny. On the whole their explanations tended towards the comic-supernatural.

'Reckon if you 'n' I, Jim 'ed gone upstairs that night, we'd 'a found a phantom waitress, all rustlin' skirts, carryin' a tray wi' wine an' wine glasses, a-goin' to do 'em in for havin' a bit o' what you fancy.'

They had a good chortle over that one. All their remarks were of that sort. They reminded me of bit parts in a particularly tedious comedy by Goldsmith or somebody. I could have sat with them all night, if I'd got that much time to waste. As it was, I turned in early.

CHAPTER 7

Family and Friends

Bill Tredgold's family lived in an unattractive suburb of Birmingham, the sort of area where people struggle valiantly with a little patch of garden, but where nature fights a losing battle against fumes and dirt, and the shadow of jerry-building. Their semi-detached probably dated from the age of Baldwin, when the virtues of Englishness were proclaimed even as England was being destroyed: thin strips of board were pasted on to stonedash, in an effort to assert tradition. At least, I thought, Bill Tredgold's short life could be seen as some sort of progress: from mock-Tudor to the real thing.

I had phoned in advance to say that I was coming, and when his father opened the door to me, he muttered:

'Don't set her off if you can help it, will you?' Their loss was clearly too recent to have been assimilated. I squeezed myself into the dim little hallway, and he led me through into the front room, which was obviously opened up for the occasion. It was cluttered with furniture, some pre- and some post-war; there were embroidered head-rests on the backs of the chairs, and a virulent orange fire of simulated logs. I edged my bulk carefully through the clutter, and sat down. The two of them sat down too, looking at me quietly but expectantly.

Both of them were in their sixties, comfortable, slightly seedy people, pleasantly without pretensions: she probably made a good steak and kidney pie, and he could fix up a shelf or mend a fuse without making a fuss about it. Small business people, perhaps, or local government office workers. The room was dotted with framed snap-shots of children and grandchildren: Bill Tredgold had not been an only child.

'So you're not satisfied either,' said Mrs Tredgold—the motherliness coming warmly through the nasal Midlands accent. 'And I must say I'm glad to hear it, because I certainly am not.'

'Now, Mother,' said her husband, for all the world as if he were in a J.B. Priestley play.

'Well, I'm not, and that's flat. And it's no good saying raking the thing up won't bring him back, because I'm not daft and I know that. That doesn't stop me wanting to get to the bottom of it all.'

'I'm interested to hear why you're not satisfied,' I said. 'Because you're quite right that I'm not.'

'Well, there was the window, for a start. The other policeman who called, he said it was tight shut. Well, a mother knows these things, and our Bill would *never* sleep with the windows closed: he'd had asthma as a child, and he always wanted them open, to get the fresh air. And don't say he might have changed, because he slept here often, when he'd been round for a meal, and it was always the same—the windows were open, winter or summer.'

'I see. Yes, that is the sort of thing people don't change their minds about. Of course, the girl could have insisted.'

'Our Bill wasn't one to take any insistence from a girl.'

'Did you know the girl?'

'Never even heard him mention the name. It's terrible, isn't it, but that's how it is these days, our Bill as well as the rest.'

'Did he tell you he was going to Knightley?'

'Not to say tell. Our Bill went all over: he was a real reporter, and we've always been that proud when we saw his name in the *Standard*, but we never knew quite where he'd be. He kept in touch, though, and by chance he did ring up the day before he died, and he mentioned then he'd be going into Shropshire.'

'But he didn't say anything more than that?'

'Not really. I just said, "Oh, on to a story, are you?" and he said, "Have you ever known me not?" '

'That's interesting. So it wasn't—well, just a night away with a girl?'

'Oh, I could tell he was on to something—he was never off duty, our Bill. If he took a holiday in Benidorm, he'd still manage to come back with something for the paper.'

'You say you hadn't heard the girl's name. Did you hear about most of his girl-friends?'

'Well, no. On the whole he kept that part of his life private.'

'We're chapel, you see,' put in Dad.

'And he was brought up in it, but somehow it just didn't stick.'

'So he didn't normally mention his girl-friends?'

'Hardly ever. Only generally, you know, because he knew we wouldn't approve. Now they say he'd been seeing a lot of this Princess Helena, at one time. You'd have thought he might have mentioned *that*, knowing we'd be interested, but he never did. I suppose you could say he was just that bit cagey-like. I suppose it came of being a reporter.'

'Perhaps—they're not the most open people. Can't afford to be. Tell me, I suppose they've sent back the things he had with him at Knightley?'

'Oh yes, after the Inquest.' She dabbed at her eyes with a little scrap of flowered handkerchief.

'Did he have the tools of his trade, so to speak, with him? Was there any sort of notebook, for example?'

She cast me a quick, intelligent look. 'No, there wasn't. I noticed at the time. It was so odd. There was hardly anything in his briefcase at all, and he never went anywhere without his notebook, because he always had two or three stories on the boil as it were. It was a sort of family joke, wasn't it, Ern, that he always had them in his trouser pocket. He used to note down things he saw, and sometimes just phrases that came into his head—might be when we were all sitting round the table at tea. And I couldn't understand why there wasn't one.'

'What about in his flat?'

She thought hard. 'Well, I'd rather forgotten by the time we went over his flat. It was sort of . . . distressing, and it went out of my mind. There *were* lots of papers: versions of stories we'd seen in the *Birmingham Standard*. And there were two notebooks—but I remember they were full ones, weren't they, Ern, because we went over them afterwards. Most of the things in them had been crossed through, after he'd used them. That was his method, to prevent him using the same phrases twice.'

'Do you still have them?'

'Oh yes, we've thrown nothing away. Get them, Ern, will you? . . . They're in his room . . . We call it his room, still. There's one other thing, Mr—'

'Trethowan.'

'Mr Trethowan. With his things from Knightley, there was a half-bottle of whisky. Unopened. Now that struck me as odd. He'd obviously brought it for the evening—you know these young people, never can be without it, I don't know why. Now, why would he go and order a bottle of wine from the hotel?'

'He didn't order one.'

'Yes, so I gathered. Well, why would he go out and buy one? As I say, I don't cotton on to the younger generation, not to their habits, but I can't see him taking a half-bottle of whisky *and* a bottle of wine with him when he goes for a night out with a lass. Can you?'

'No,' I said, 'I can't.'

'I've got the notebooks,' said Ern Tredgold, coming back into the dowdy little sitting-room, 'and I thought you might like these: they were in his flat—seems like they're the articles he was working on when he died.'

I took the sheaf of papers he had in his hand, and the two fat, thumbed little notebooks, suitable for slipping into trouser pockets. I stood up to go.

'I hope they'll be of help,' said Ern Tredgold; and then, rather hesitantly, 'We would both like to be of help, Mother and I. It isn't that I wanted to throw cold water on it. I know Mother will be upset, but still we'd both rather know how he died, if there was anything wrong in it.'

'Of course we want to know,' said Elsie Tredgold, more robustly. 'The trouble with you is, you'd rather let sleeping dogs lie, even when it's your own son as has been killed.'

'It's just that I haven't wanted you upset, Mother . . .'

'I'd be more upset being in doubt . . .' She opened the door for me, and I edged my way out into the dim winter sunshine. 'You *will* get to the bottom of it, won't you, Mr Trethowan? We love all our children, naturally, but he was—well, he was the pride of them. He was so bright, and sharp as a razor, and that cheerful with it. There wasn't anything he couldn't have done. He could have been editor of *The Times*!'

A mother might have wished a safer long-term prospect on her son than that, but I took her point. I had every reason to think Bill Tredgold had been a first-rate reporter.

I won't inflict on you in detail my conversation with Carol Crossley's family, or her flatmate. The family was the sort that washes its hands so enthusiastically of its young when they reach maturity that you wonder why they had kids in the first place. They hadn't seen Carol for three months or more before she died, and they did not seem to have expected to. For what it was worth, they agreed with her flatmate that she had no discernible enemies. I got the impression of a nineteen-year-old shorthand typist, with no very strong personality and a rather aimless existence. I found it almost impossible to believe that she—in her own person, rather than as the Princess surrogate—was the intended victim. She did, however, look a little like Helena, but mainly in the sort of way girls started looking like the Princess of Wales as soon as the engagement was announced. It was clear from her flatmate's account that she slept around a bit, though hardly frenetically. I asked about her relationship with Bill Tredgold.

'I'd never heard the name before the inquest. Honest. It was dead embarrassing, in a way. Nor had the other girls in her office. Makes her look so cheap, doesn't it? But I was away the day before, and it's my bet she met him on the Thursday night, and he persuaded her to get off work early on Friday and go away with him for the weekend. She liked that sort of offer, because she loved travelling, and you don't feel you're giving it away for free then, do you?'

'Did she close the window at night?'

'I beg your pardon?'

'When she slept, did she like the window open or closed?'

'Oh, sorry—misunderstood. Well, normally she'd have it open, unless it was really freezing.'

So there it was. As far as I could see, Carol Crossley was a casual pick-up of Bill Tredgold's, someone to take on a trip he'd already decided on, and not someone to insist on their closing their window on their night of love. I felt sorry for the poor girl: rarely has a casual night's sex led to such immediate retribution.

More useful, from my point of view, was a conversation I had with one of Bill Tredgold's fellow reporters. This chap had shared an office with Bill at the *Standard*'s headquarters, and like him he was young and eager—he hadn't got that dingy, hollow-chested, nicotine-stained look of the reporter who's been on the game all too long. I suppose he was on the way there, though, because I had to take him to the nearest pub and buy him two or three pints before I really got him to open up.

'He was a bright boy, Bill,' he said, gulping down thirstily, and wiping his mouth with the back of his hand in a *Coronation Street* kind of way. 'Quick. Bright. The sort of chap you could see would make his way to the top. Barring accidents. He could smell out a story at a hundred paces. You could practically see his nose quivering. That's why the *Guardian* was interested. He'd had several first-rate Specials on the *Standard*—immigrant housing, illiteracy, battered wives—all good *Guardian* stuff. But he wasn't just social conscience: he did a first-rate piece on the Solihull child molester, and last year he did a series on municipal corruption. There was a city councillor had to resign over that one, even if they did call it "ill health". The *Standard*'s missing him already, because he was a first-rate all-round reporter.'

'Do you know what he was working on when he died?'

'A young lass called Carol—sorry, shouldn't joke about that. Still, it was a bit *Tristan and Isolde*, wasn't it? Bill would have burst his sides if it had been one of his stories. Sorry, I've forgotten what you asked me.'

'What was he working on when he died?'

'Haven't a clue. We're reporters, remember: we don't go handing each other scoops. He was damned excited about whatever it was, I do know that.'

'Oh?'

'Well, he said one day, over a pint it was, this very pub, he said: "I don't know whether to offer this thing I'm on now to the *Standard*, as a last gesture, because they've been good to me, or sit on it and give it to the *Guardian*." '

'What did he decide?'

'I don't think he had. But he did say it ought to go to the *Guardian*, because it was a national thing, not just a local one.'

'It wasn't something he'd been assigned to?'

'Oh no. We all have jobs like that, the things that take up most of our normal working time. This was something he'd nosed out for himself—that was why he was secretive about it, that's why he could offer it to the *Guardian*. He used to call it Operation Seneca. Those were practically the last words I heard him speak, as a matter of fact. That was lunch-time Friday: I asked him what he was doing over the weekend: "I'm fully employed with Operation Seneca," he said. I chaffed him a bit about working his tripes out to get on the *Guardian*, and he said: "Oh, Operation Seneca isn't all work. I always manage to combine a spot of pleasure with business when I'm on that little job." Next thing I heard he was dead.'

Well, that was about all I got out of my second day with the Princess in the Midlands. In the afternoon I went back on duty, to Joplin's intense relief. He had had to endure all manner of dire official visits and charity receptions, quite apart from the Beckett, but all I had was the Birmingham premiere of a new Christie film, in aid of the Civil Service Widows' Benevolent Fund. The Princess asked me in the middle who'd done it, and I told her, and in the train going back to London I gave her my chain of reasoning. I didn't tell her I'd read the book anyway. Lady Dorothy said personally she preferred Dorothy Sayers, which didn't surprise me one little bit. Anyway, the Princess and I were rather light-hearted and jolly, and (not to put too fine a point on it) getting on like a house on fire.

Of course, we weren't to know we were travelling back to another murder.

CHAPTER 8

By His Own Hand?

With the exception of one royal engagement, the next day was devoted entirely to research. That one engagement was a football match, and there is not a lot to say about it, except for one thing I noticed about the Princess: she was not only delighted when she evoked admiration and applause, she was also adept at augmenting it. She was like nothing so much as Callas at curtain-call. She timed her entry for the precise psychological moment to get most attention, she feigned most subtly a sort of humility, and as she stood there acknowledging the raucous, good-humoured (and possibly jollily obscene) cheers and claps, she had one or two little gestures which touched the heart and screwed enthusiasm up to fever pitch—an uncertain movement of the hand to the breast, expressive of modesty and pleasure, though I suspected it was actually neither uncertain nor modest, and in fact it was a movemen which helped to show off the gorgeous form of the girl t perfection. Artful little minx. I wondered if the Quee went in for these admiration-stimulators, but rathe doubted it.

The Princess's comments on the game were knowl edgeable, but mostly of the private lives of the players gleaned, I suppose, from the narrations of their bedtim tactics and scores purveyed by their ex-wives an mistresses to the readership of the *Daily Grub*. Me, I wa so much on duty, and the Princess Helena was so muc exposed, that I hardly noticed what went on on the field and was even uncertain at the end who had won. Th Princess shook a lot of sweaty and dirty paws with obviou interest, exchanged a very meaningful look with one o the players, and then we all drove home.

Otherwise, as I say, I spent the day going into th journalistic career of Bill Tredgold. I picked up a whol pile of relevant stuff at the Yard, and then took it all bac to the flat to go over it with Jan. It was her last day hom before she and Daniel went back for Spring term a Newcastle, and we settled down by the fire with it an had a real cosy day.

As his mother had said, the notebooks they ha retrieved from Bill's room were old—or rather they wer used up. Most of the entries had been crossed through either because they were no go, or because he had use them in one or other of his articles. I checked the against a volume of back issues of the *Birminghar Standard*, and it seemed that the notebooks covered period roughly from late September to early November o the previous year. Bill had had a series of five article called 'Failures of the Welfare State' printed around tha time, and a lot of the entries had been used in those Sometimes the entries were just phrases, sometimes the were stories relevant to his theme—the mistreate children that social workers had shut their eyes to, the lonely dead who remained undiscovered for months, the hospitals run down to the point of being insanitary, the schools without textbooks or equipment—the shabby, all-too-common stories which somehow seem to sum up Britain today. Some of the entries referred to news stories he had been assigned to—from allegations of police brutality to incredible talking parrots. Often there were notes suggesting plans for a later follow-up story, but there would be none of those now.

Then there were the entries which remained uncrossed through. Some of these, I thought, could hardly have any bearing on the threat to the Princess: 'Check on Councillor Duxbury's connection with Midland Building Enterprises'—that sort of thing. If I came to the conclusion that Bill Tredgold's death had been the result of his investigations into civic corruption, then I'd hand the whole thing over to the Birmingham police and wash my hands of it.

But there was one entry that puzzled me, and which I could not dismiss so lightly. It was nothing more than a list of places, one after the other:

Oldham
Nuneaton
Cumberland
Leamington
Stourbridge

There was nothing there to pull me up. For all I knew it could be Bill Tredgold's plans for future dirty weekends (no, not Oldham, surely). But what did intrigue me was the pencilled entry in the margin: OS.

'Well, it can hardly mean "outsize",' said Jan, and I enlightened her on Operation Seneca.

But if it did refer to that, what on earth could be the significance of such a list? Four of the places were roughly speaking Midlands to Northern, and all within fairly easy reach of Birmingham (Oldham being farthest away). But none of them was particularly close to Knightley, where he died. And what in the world was Cumberland doing there?

Two lines down from this list, underlined, was the word 'Treasurer', but I could not decide whether it had any connection, or was related to a case of civic bribery which was the entry immediately below.

Jan and I chewed over all this as we went through it, and then again after Daniel had been despatched to bed, but beyond the fact that we both had the impression of Bill Tredgold as a bright boy and a sympathetic personality—committed, involved, yet thoroughly practical and down-to-earth—we could make little of it. On the other hand, I had that itching feeling that there was a connection there, waiting to be made, and I had no doubt that if we could lay our hands on any subsequent notebook we would probably find the vital clue to the whole business. But where was that now? Ashes, I wouldn't mind betting. It was a pretty funny way for Jan and me to spend our last evening together, but policemen don't lead normal lives, as a rule, and neither do policemen's wives.

I went over all this again the next morning in the car with Joplin as we drove to the Palace. We had met up at Scotland Yard, where I had found the message 'Bayle, Basin Street, nine-thirty' waiting for me. So last night the Princess had been with her Parliamentary friend. That was worth knowing. I made arrangements to have any future messages of the kind sent to me at home, and I made a mental note to get Jeremy Styles to perform a similar service. I had no illusions about the Honourable Edwin Frere co-operating, and rather doubted whether she would be so much in his company in future.

That day the Princess was free, at any rate of official duties. On the other hand, if she should decide to go anywhere privately, it would be best if she could be persuaded to take somebody with her. On the way in Joplin and I had a word with the cop on duty at the barrier which shielded the residential part of Kensington Palace from the gazes of the vulgar. He had seen nothing suspicious, beyond an amiable crackpot who had been in love with Princess Margaret since 1956; he had been loitering there to watch her drive past on her way to visit the Royal Ballet School. He had been checked out scores of times over the years, without result. I thought it rather to his credit that he hadn't transferred his hopeless affections to any of the younger royal ladies.

I drove through into the courtyard, and Joplin and I separated, he to take over some of the security jobs at the Palace door, I to go through and check whether the Princess had any personal plans for the day. Once more (I was getting used to it) I was taken through the dark wooden corridors by the fair young footman I'd seen on the first day. He replied in monosyllables to my attempt at relaxed conversation. Well, it wasn't much of an attempt: relaxed conversation did not flow easily in that rather overcast environment.

Eventually we arrived at the chilly antechamber which had become familiar if hardly welcoming since we had talked to the Princess's private secretary there on our first visit to the Palace. Once again the typist was busy in the corner—Miss Trimble her name was, I had found out, and a tight-lipped scrap of gentility she was to be sure. I seldom got more out of her than I had done that first day, but I assumed my most ingratiating manner as I went over to her rickety little desk.

'Ah, Miss Trimble, a cold sort of morning, isn't it? The Princess is free today, I believe, isn't she?'

'Yes, she is.'

'Do you happen to know whether she plans to go out anywhere informally?'

'She would be unlikely to tell me.' Lips pursed: and I would be the last to expect it, she seemed to say. 'Perhaps Mr Brudenell knows, but he has not yet arrived—'

But at that moment the Princess herself danced in, and you could see she had no engagements: jeans, no less, and a tight-fitting silk blouse that emphasized everything that her official dresses only gave tantalizing hints of. I say jeans, but these jeans were to work denims what a Fabergé Easter egg is to the kids' chocolate variety. They were svelte, I tell you: they hugged her all the way, and she looked like a Sunday Supplement fashion plate.

'Oh—hello, Superintendent. How *awful* we're not going out together today. Perhaps I could think of something for after lunch. We've both been so *busy* I've hardly begun to get to know you. Miss Trimble, tell Mr Brudenell I'm ready to go through the correspondence, will you?'

'I'm afraid Mr Brudenell hasn't arrived yet, Your Royal Highness.'

She looked at the desiccated little secretary with arrogant incomprehension.

'Hasn't arrived? But I said I'd see him at eleven.'

'I'm very sorry, Ma'am—'

'Hasn't he sent a message?' I asked.

'I haven't received one. I'll check again with the Household and see if one has come in.'

'This is awfully inconvenient,' pouted the Princess, turning to me. 'I suppose there's some silly demonstration or other holding up the traffic.'

'The traffic was running perfectly normally a few minutes ago, Ma'am. Does Mr Brudenell have far to drive?'

'Oh no. I've been there. South Kensington somewhere. No distance.' She drummed her fingers on the table as Miss Trimble spoke into the 'phone. She looked like a spoiled debutante whose Delight has stood her up.

'They've had no word through, Ma'am. I'll ring his flat, shall I?'

But as the ringing went on and on, I began to get more and more uneasy.

'Has this ever happened before, Ma'am?'

'Never,' she said emphatically.

'I'm going round,' I said. 'Miss Trimble, what's his address?'

'Whitehaven Mansions, Lichfield Street.'

'Will there be some kind of caretaker?'

'Oh yes, it's a very—'

'Ring him and tell him we're coming. Tell him we may need the key to Brudenell's flat.'

And I made my way to the door with a near total lack of ceremony. As I went through it, I heard the Princess say: 'Really, it's not *that* important.'

The thought flashed through my mind: does she really think I'm just worried about the inconvenience to her of her secretary missing his appointment? Is she really so dim? But the thought went from me as I raced through the corridors, flinging off the fair iceberg of a flunkey, and out into the courtyard.

'Joplin!' I shouted. 'The car.'

And we slid in and sped out into Kensington Palace Gardens and negotiated the stream of traffic in Kensington High Street, going in the direction of Lichfield Street.

In the car I had to explain to Joplin what was up, and when I began to do so, it began to sound lame. Someone being late for work, it wasn't more than that.

'Call it a hunch,' I said finally. 'But there is some basis for it. He's a precise, pernickety little piece of nothing very much—well, you saw what he's like: formal, meticulous, devoted to doing the right thing. If he was just sick he'd ring up with apologies, special messages of regret to the Princess, the lot. Helena says it's never happened before, and I can believe it. Of course, there could have been a traffic accident—'

We drew up outside the Mansions: luxury pads for private incomes, built in the 'thirties, I would guess, anonymously smooth in style, but with a sort of decaying smugness. Once, I suppose, they would have had a uniformed attendant looking impressive in the main entrance. Now there was just a caretaker, grey and not too clean, who stood at the door waiting for us.

'Mr Brudenell, is it? It's the third floor, number two. Here's the key.'

'Have you seen him today?'

'Not today, no. But I've been busy out the back, and I didn't think twice. Usually he's very regular. Sails by at ten, with never a pleasant word for a body. But you can set your watch by him, as a rule.'

We took the lift up, and ran through the thickly carpeted corridor to number two. The air was heavy with frigid gentility and money from dividends. The bell produced no result, and we opened up. The door led into a hallway, papered in Regency stripe, with little round embroidered pictures and prints of a tasteful sort. I called out, into the plushy silence. No reply. I pushed open what seemed to be the main door, and found myself in a sitting-room—large, velvety, lacking in personality, but with capacious armchairs and sofa. Pictures by Paul Nash. I glanced around, then walked across the room and pushed open a door to the right. The study. All the walls lined with books—red-bound autobiographies, middle-brow novels in hardback, an encyclopædia, *Burke's Peerage*. They dominated the room. So much so that you could almost overlook the natty little desk towards the far corner, with the typewriter neatly in place in the centre. Except that now it had a body, sprawling grotesquely sideways across it.

It was Brudenell, of course. Still looking a bit like a

pouter pigeon, shot by some maniac for fouling Nelson's Column perhaps, his fat little belly still poked under the desk, his bottom pushed through the back of the chair. He had been shot, that much was clear. Though he was still sitting at his desk he had fallen to the right, his right arm under him, his face resting on the green leather desktop. A small enamelled pistol, almost a toy, had fallen to the floor, apparently from his left hand. There was a neat little hole in the left side of his head.

'Almost like a stage-set, isn't it?' said Joplin. 'What's the betting it isn't suicide?'

I wasn't taking him on. I sent him down to the caretaker, so that he could call to the Yard from there. Fingerprints are a forlorn hope these days, but you have to make ritual bows in the direction of that possibility. He scooted off, and meanwhile I tiptoed round the study, getting my bearings.

The first thing that I saw was the top drawer of the desk on the left-hand side—it was left open, while all the others were neatly closed, as one would expect of Mr Brudenell. The scenario was obvious: Mr James Brudenell, sitting at his typewriter, takes a gun from the drawer and shoots himself on an impulse. That was what we were meant to think, and I may say I found it a thoroughly unlikely scenario. Brudenell as a possible suicide I could accept, but not on an impulse: I doubt whether he did anything without fussy preliminaries. He was the sort who would write a letter to the Coroner, and worry about the correct form of address.

The body had fallen clear of the typewriter, and I walked carefully over and looked at the sheet of paper still sticking out of the machine. It was headed typing paper, with the Whitehaven Mansions address at the top, and what was being written was a letter:

Dear John,

I must tell you, with great regret, that I can no

longer continue giving way to the monstrous financial demands you

There was no address for the recipient. Presumably, therefore, an intimate, if not a friend. I continued cautiously circling the room. On the far side of the desk the bullet had singed a track, finally lodging in the floor under the bookshelves. I stood considering the desk and shook my head, dissatisfied. It didn't add up, I felt sure. Or rather, what it added up to was a strong smell of fish. Someone had been too clever by half.

'They're on their way,' said Joplin, coming back into the flat.

'Good,' I shouted. 'Come through, Garry. Have a look here. It's obvious what the set-up is, as we're meant to understand it. Brudenell is typing. Reply to a blackmail demand. He takes the gun from the drawer, and shoots himself. The bullet singes the edge of the desk, and lodges—over here, right? Into the floor. Now, before the other boys arrive, look around. Anything else you notice in this room that I haven't spotted?'

As I said before, Joplin has marvellous, sharp little eyes. He stalked cautiously round the room, darting them about. He shook his head over the letter in the typewriter, noticed the bullet mark, and then finally came to rest by a good-sized side table in the opposite corner of the room. It was empty, and had a large easy chair beside it. I followed his eyes.

'Yes, I see,' I said. 'Good lad.'

Most of the furniture in the room was covered by a light film of dust. I guessed that Brudenell employed a char a couple of days a week, and no doubt tut-tutted impotently at the inefficiency of her operations, and regretted the time when chars could be made to work their fingers to the bone for a pittance. This round table, however, had that film of dust only on the very edges: there was a large, square area in the centre that was hardly dusty at all. We stood looking at it.

'Now what,' I pondered aloud, 'was lying there, and lying there until recently? A newspaper? One doesn't lay a newspaper down on a table to read it. A book? The area's much too big—unless it was something like an atlas. An atlas . . .'

I suddenly remembered Bill Tredgold's list of places, and wondered if by some chance or process of reasoning Brudenell had come by the same knowledge, or was conjecturing along the same lines. I would have gone to the bookshelves, but I wanted to leave the room to the fingerprint men, and there were other things to do first. As I was thinking, they all arrived—the technicians of death, and a posse of regular men from the Yard. McPhail, the Princess's erstwhile and dour security man, had been put on the case, which was a sensible enough decision. Capable, if hardly exciting. He looked round the room as if it sunk him into a profound gloom, and then started getting on with the job in the careful, efficient way I knew so well

I left him to it: I thought that the less the present protector of the Princess had to do with the investigation the better, at least as far as the newspapers were concerned. But I had a word with him before I went, and pointed out the dustless shape on the table. I wanted it measured and marked. Then Joplin and I hot-footed it back to the Palace.

I immediately asked to see the lady-in-waiting, and in that cold, bare antechamber told her (and incidentally and inevitably Miss Trimble as well) the essentials of the matter. Lady Dorothy blinked her concern, and gave little strangulated expressions of shock in the course of my narrative.

'As far as we can see at the moment,' I ended, 'he committed suicide. But that is only a preliminary judgement, of course.'

'How absolutely frightful,' she drawled. 'Quit
appalling. I had no idea . . . Was he *ill*, or something?
'That we shall hope to find out,' I said.

'You'll tell the Princess, of course,' she said.

That I had rather hoped to get her to do, but she said i
in so definitive a way that it almost seemed that som
rigid point of etiquette might be involved (a Roya
Personage shall always be informed by her Securit
Officer in the event of her Private Secretary putting
bullet in himself—that kind of thing). So I didn't argu
the toss, but meekly assented, and after a hushed tele
phone conversation I gathered the Princess would receiv
me. I was taken straight through to her sitting-room, an
there she was, stretched out in those glorious jeans alon
her sofa, reading a glossy magazine and listening to Ro
Stewart in loud stereo. She did not turn him down, but a
soon as her lady-in-waiting withdrew she turned an
smiled at me invitingly.

'Your Royal Highness, I'm afraid I have some bad new
for you. When I got to his flat, I found Mr Brudenel
dead.'

'Good Lord,' she said, gaping at me prettily. 'Ho
extraordinarily sudden!'

'It seems he may have committed suicide.'

'Oh *really*!' she said pettishly, as if mainly struc
by the inconsiderateness of the action. 'What an awfu
bore!'

To relieve Mr Brudenell's shade of the burden of roya
displeasure I perhaps foolishly added: 'That's how it look
at the moment. But I'm afraid we can't rule out the possibility of foul play.'

'Foul play? Do you mean murder?'

I nodded. 'It is just a remote possibility.'

'But how fascinating!' And she gazed at me with a catlike smile on her face and repeated her earlier excla
mation of delighted anticipation: 'Frightfully exciting!'

CHAPTER 9

Scene of the Crime

The Princess realized almost at once the effect she had made on me with her reception of the news, and for some reason she thought it worth while to try to soften the impression.

'Of course, it's quite *awful*,' she said, swivelling round her splendid legs to get herself into a sitting position, and then gazing at me with a sincere and concerned expression on her face. 'He was *terribly* loyal, you know? and quite sweet in his way. He's given me an *awful* lot of good advice and all that, these last two or three years, I mean how to behave and all that, and how to pretend to be interested, which is really an *art*, I can tell you, and he knew all the tricks . . . Still, I mean, he wasn't quite *human*, was he? Hardly a *man*, would you say? So prissy and correct, you sometimes felt he belonged in another century. More at home with Queen Anne, or somebody. I'm awfully *concerned*, naturally, but you can't expect me to *care*, can you? Not *per*sonally, I mean.'

And on thinking it over, I didn't suppose I could. Her first reaction had at least been natural and sincere, much more sincere than her assumed sincerity. It did seem rather a poor return for Mr Brudenell's years of service. But it was typical of her that her thoughts were already turning to the future.

'Actually, I shall probably regret him like hell in a week or two. I mean Aunty will probably inflict somebody much worse on me. The thing was, I could run rings around him, but heaven knows *who* they'll send from the Palace now. Of course it would be lovely if it was someone really *dishy*, but I'm quite sure it won't be: nobody dishy would take a job like this, and if there was somebody, they wouldn't give him to me. No, I bet it will be some *gaoler*, you know? Someone who won't give me a *moment*'s freedom. Because they probably don't trust me an *inch*.'

I sincerely hoped she was right, but I only said: 'So you don't appoint your own Private Secretary?'

'Oh *no*. Not on your life. Well, perhaps *officially* I do, but they have *ways*.'

She made it sound terribly like the KGB, but I must say that in this case I saw the point of the Powers That Be. I (treacherously) decided to have a word with someone at the Palace, and suggest the qualities I thought desirable in Mr Brudenell's successor: not a gaolor, exactly, but a damned good animal trainer. Cherishing this thought, I took a ceremonious leave.

'You will keep me totally informed, won't you?' was the Princess's parting shot. 'Fancy being in on a murder!'

As I passed through Miss Trimble's antechamber I had a word with her, telling her to inform whoever was at the moment in charge of the Household that I would need an office somewhere in the Princess's quarters. Then, as usual, I was flunkied out.

Flunkied out, in fact, by little South Pole—the chilly, fair-haired youth who had interrupted my first talk with Mr James Brudenell. I remembered Joplin's succinct summing up of what he imagined the situation between those two to be, and in the brown-wooded, lowering corridors I stopped and turned to him. His reluctance to talk flashed momentarily over his face, almost the first sign of emotion I had seen him emit.

'You've heard the news, I suppose?' I said.

A pause, the significance of which I could not determine. Respectful? A rebuke?

'Mr Brudenell's death? Yes, sir. Extremely tragic, sir.'

'You knew Mr Brudenell well?'

'Naturally, sir. He was a member of the Household. He was here every day.'

I could of course have pressed him further, but I decided to leave it at that for the moment.

'I shall need to talk to members of the staff here,' I said. 'Do you go off duty in the evening?'

'I personally, sir? No, I am on duty this evening. I shall sleep at the Palace . . . Excuse me, sir, but does this mean—?'

'Yes?'

'Does this mean you're not . . . satisfied?'

'The case has to come before the Coroner, as I'm sure you realize. The police have to collect all the facts for the inquest. I don't think you should read anything more into it than that.'

'I see, sir. Thank you, sir.'

Quite respectful he was becoming. We resumed our stately egress from the Palace.

I spent the afternoon at the Yard, getting the details of the investigation as they were sent me by McPhail and his squad. They were the standard stuff of the first hours of an investigation. I also had a word with Buckingham Palace, made an appointment with one of the high-ups there, and suggested—greatly daring—that the Princess should be advised to lie very low as far as her private life was concerned for the next few days: it would do nobody any good if she were photographed at a disco on the day her Private Secretary died. The suggestion was received cordially enough, but I think they had thought of it already.

But what I mainly spent the time on that afternoon was delving into the background of James Brudenell. James Eliot Macpherson Brudenell, to be precise.

It was a sad little story, really. He had come of a fairly good family (which I suppose is like saying of a dog that it's nearly a pedigree). His father was an Old Harrovian, a sporty type and a high liver, without the income to support his tastes in style. He had acquired a wife and child before he had acquired the ability to hold down a job. He had departed for the Colonies in 1953, intending to bring out his family when he had established himself. But he had no sooner established himself than he had abandoned the intention of bringing out his family. He had been variously a mining executive, a farmer, a Rhodesian Front MP, and was currently in the service of the Emir of Onan (a state in which the Moslem proprieties were rigorously observed, and where a snifter and a bit of skirt must have been grievously hard to come by).

His wife and son, meanwhile, lived in a fairly miserable little semi-detached in Blackheath, on the irregular remittances received from husband and father. A wealthy relative, however, helped with the boy's education, and he had attended a nearby preparatory school, and later been a day boy at St Paul's. He was, by all accounts, a cosseted, well-wrapped-up, excessively mothered child. At school he was predictably miserable, having none of the qualities that made for popularity, nor even any that might have given him a small circle of chosen friends. After an undistinguished university career (a third in history from Oriel), he had got himself a job with the College of Heralds—concocting shields for Labour life peers and that sort of thing. After undertaking some special job in the library of Balmoral, cataloguing Queen Victoria's laundry lists or something, he had gone on to the strength at Clarence House. Thence he had come, rather over two years before, to his present position.

Of private life he had had, apparently, none. He had lived with his mother until a legacy, and shortly afterwards her death, had released him from her increasingly querulous thrall and enabled him to purchase a more eligible address. He seemed to have made little use of his new freedoms. In spite of Joplin's conjecture, he had never been suspected of homosexual offences (but then the law had been changed when he was about twenty, so that, provided he made sure he didn't fancy anyone under the magic age of twenty-one, there was no reason why he should be). In any case, if there had been anything of that kind on the records against him, he would certainly not have got his present job. On the other hand, I did wonder whether the Palace had decided that a decently repressed homosexual was just the type needed for a position in the Princess Helena's household.

His tastes in the wider sense were unexceptionable. He enjoyed a first night at the theatre, on those now rare occasions when a good middle-brow play was to be presented. He sometimes went to the opera, but apparently more for social reasons than musical: he only went to Covent Garden, and one suspected his chief pleasure was in the little supper parties he arranged for after the performance. He was a member of the Monarchist League, and did amateur research work for Debrett and suchlike works. He inserted a memorial notice ever year in *The Times* for Tsar Ferdinand of Bulgaria ('of pious and glorious memory') between whom and his own family his genealogical ingenuity had discovered a connection. His club was the dullest in London, he had forsworn all political affiliations since Oxford, and he had no close friends as far as anybody knew. A sad, comic, ineffectual little life.

I got the same feeling, later in the day, when I went back with Joplin to his Kensington flat. The photographers and dabs-men had done their work, and the body had been removed to the hygienic anonymity of the morgue. We felt ourselves now more free of the place, and could walk around without holding our breaths, as we had done in the morning. McPhail had kept me posted during the day, and had considerately left us a photocopy of the letter in the typewriter, as well as a note with some of the technicalities of the scientific part of the investigation usefully detailed. The char, we gathered, had been interviewed, and had sworn that the gun used was Brudenell's, and had been kept in the upper left-hand drawer that we had found open. She and all who knew him swore that he was indeed left-handed. The char had not been in since Monday, but the week before she had done a premature spring-clean: there were consequently very few prints in the flat except hers and Brudenell's. The caretaker, who was only around during the day, had known nothing of any regular visitors to Brudenell's flat, and, like the char, had rather suspected that there were none. The Princess and Lady Dorothy had once come to tea, and a great fuss and kerfuffle had been made about that by Brudenell. But that was months ago, and the visit had not been repeated. ('Thank God. The silly little runt practically disappeared up his own backside with the excitement of it,' said the caretaker.)

I strolled around the study looking at the books. Brudenell's tastes in fiction had been staid and rather dated: there were Charles Morgan, Rosamond Lehmann, Pamela Hansford-Johnson, and the first three volumes in Anthony Powell's Music of Time sequence. There were standard biographies, particularly of monarchs: Cecil Woodham-Smith on Victoria, Wedgwood on Charles I, Ziegler on William IV. A lot of Antonia Frasers. There was a whole shelf of royal memoirs—you know the sort of thing: *My Memories of Twenty-Five Reigns*, by the Princess Augusta-Alexandrina of Hohenlau-Stauffenberg. Style a cross between a *Daily Telegraph* leader and a novel by Denise Robins, the whole stuffed with pictures of Nicky and Alicky at Tsarskoe Selo, or Willy and Sophy cruising in the Norwegian fjords. Signing sessions at Harrods in the week of publication, remaindered in the

Charing Cross Road six months later. But Mr Brudenell, I felt sure, paid the full price, as he no doubt also did for the unrevealing memoirs of Conservative politicians of the old school or the immensely tedious memoirs of noble personages from the shires, though one of these (*Hounds and Horn in the Morning*) was personally inscribed to him in the not-very-literate hand of the author.

So far, so predictable.

I went to the desk, across which Brudenell's body had lately slumped, and took up a copy of the dead man's last letter.

'It's obvious what we are meant to think,' I said to Joplin, who strolled in from a sniff around the kitchen. 'Poor old Brudenell has been having it off with some boy or other, and the boy has been milking him for some time. Suddenly the whole business becomes intolerable, and he decides to end it all. Takes the pistol which he conveniently keeps for such emergencies in the left hand drawer, and bang! the soul of Brudenell J. is launched into eternity. Very neat little plot indeed. Why then do I get a whiff of week-old kippers?'

'For a start, why give in to blackmail?' said Joplin. 'Blackmailing queers is dead as a dodo. It's not against the law.'

'But it's not that,' I said. 'Because you could imagine Brudenell giving way, in his position: the threat would be not "I'll go to the Police", but "I'll go to the Palace". The mere hint of anything unsavoury and he'd be gently eased out. But look here, if he'd been shacking up with some desirable plumber's mate who'd then been putting the finger on him over a longish period, would he begin a letter to him with "I must tell you with great regret—".'

'Well, Brudenell might,' said Joplin dubiously.

'No, he wouldn't. Not to a social inferior. He might to a scion of the nobility, but why would such a chap go with Brudenell? He had no obvious attractions, nor any subtle ones, I would have said. It would have to be some sordid little affair, entered into on the other chap's part either for money or some other material inducement.'

'Fair point, I suppose,' said Joplin. 'I wonder what that footman's name is.'

'We'll find out later tonight. I've lined him up for an interview. What I'm looking forward to is the lab boy's report on this letter. And on the machine too. I wouldn't mind betting—'

'What?'

'That up to the word "continue" or thereabouts, there is one hand typing, and that "giving way to the monstrous financial demands you" was typed by a different hand, with different pressure on the keys.'

'It was an electric machine. Would it show?'

'Probably, if whoever it was was being careful about fingerprints. It would be less confident, because he wouldn't want to smudge over Brudenell's prints. Yes, I'm looking forward to the report on the keys, even if he used gloves, which he surely must have. Hmm. Most of the letters appear in both halves of the sentence, but "d" only appears in the second half, and "j" in the first. I think I'll tell McPhail to pay particular attention to those. Then there's the switching-off mechanism . . .'

So I got on to the phone to the dour little man, now back at the Yard, and had a bit of a natter—that is, I nattered to him, and he uttered soft little grunts of agreement. But he did tell me one thing, and when I rang off I relayed it to Joplin.

'Gun not registered in this country. Apparently bought in the States. Natty little job, as you saw, with enamelled porcelain handle. Perhaps he thought it amusing. It's the sort of thing American ladies buy if they want to have a go at muggers, rapists or Presidents. Anyway, it did for Brudenell quite as effectively as a more manly instrument.'

'Those Americans are gun-mad,' said Joplin.

'The bullet,' I went on, 'certainly came from that gun. The ballistics people said there was no question at all of hat. But what gets me is the angle of the bullet.' I went back to the desk. 'See—he's sitting *here*: the bullet goes *down*, so it grazes the edge of the desk, *down* still into the kirting-board under the bookcase. Now, if that scenario ve just sketched out was valid, Brudenell would stop yping, reach for the gun, and *surely* when he did that he vould have to straighten up. The bullet would go along o hit the books in the case, or it might go slightly *up*, but urely it wouldn't go *down*.'

'That puzzled me,' said Joplin. 'As it is—'

'As it is, it looks for all the world as if he were shot while ie was typing, by someone standing above him. How did vhoever it was get hold of the gun? Was Brudenell ntirely unsuspicious? Did he say nothing when the visitor eached over and got it? Did he keep on typing until he let iim have it? Why was Brudenell typing at all in his isitor's presence? Hardly the thing, by Brudenell's lights, would have thought. Still, I can imagine answers to hose questions. What I can't imagine is Brudenell yping, grabbing the gun, remaining hunched over his ypewriter, and shooting himself *from above*, the hand oised *over* the head, so that the bullet went downwards nto the floor over there in the corner.'

'I presume McPhail isn't happy either.'

'Not at all. He's got all his wits, even if they don't seem o send messages to his tongue. I see his men have marked out that space on the table that you noticed.'

We walked over to it, and looked at it together.

'Of course it could be nothing,' I said. 'What he iappened to be reading yesterday evening—the death occurred around midnight, give or take a couple of hours either way. It's the size of the space that puzzles me. It doesn't seem to correspond with any sort of book I know.

Where's his atlas—that seems most likely.'

We searched through the shelves, and finally came up with the *Edinburgh World Atlas*.

'Not big enough by a long way. What else is there?'

We came to a shelf of books too big to go in the normal cases. There were glossy books about stately homes, books of heraldic interest, a book of Hockney reproductions, and a two volume work on Royal Families of the World ('Bokhassa, Emperor, crowned 1976' and so on). All of them were weighty tomes, at least in the literal sense, but none of them was big enough to cover the space.

'Odd,' I said. 'It really must have been a *hell* of a big book. And yet a newspaper would surely be *too* big. Here, there's a *Times* in my briefcase. Try it.'

But it was too big by far. We went through every shelf, and even tried the odd file on his desk for size. It was when we had given up for the night and were walking vaguely disconsolately through the sitting-room that I spotted it.

'I say, look there, Garry. Isn't that about what we're looking for?'

Down beside one of the armchairs near the hearth was a series of shelves, intended for periodicals and newspapers. But on the bottom shelf were three very large books, bound in dark red leather. I took hold of the top one gingerly. They were scrapbooks, specially made, and inside were pasted pictures of the Princess Helena on her various public appearances, as well as family portraits and other such mementoes of her. It seemed that Mr Brudenell was sentimental about the activities of his mistress, or perhaps took a certain pride in his part in her career. I took the enormous scrapbook back into the study and laid it down on the table. It fitted exactly.

Then I got on the phone to McPhail and told him to put his boys on to it.

CHAPTER 10

Young Woodley

When finally we got back to Kensington Palace, towards ten in the evening, I did a very traditional thing: I sent Joplin below stairs to talk to the Palace staff, while I had a private interview with young South Pole, up in the eaves. It was a bedroom without any character, one that was used by any member of the staff who happened to be on duty. There was a Utility bed, and several sticks of furniture that looked as if they had been discarded by William or Mary. No doubt I would have got a more definite impression of the fair footman if I had interviewed him at home. As it was, he sat on the bed in footman's trousers and open-necked shirt, his manner apparently courteous and concerned, masking an undertow of hostility and suspicion.

'Your name is—?'

'Malcolm Woodley.'

'And you've been in service here in the Palace— ?'

'A little over a year.'

'I see. And did Mr Brudenell engage you?'

'Oh no, sir. Mr Brudenell had nothing to do with the domestic arrangements.'

As well as a desire to distance himself from Brudenell there was also a slight superciliousness in his reply, as if any fool knew about the organization of a royal household. It riled me.

'And were you already sleeping with him when you were engaged?'

I often find a direct approach pays dividends, and it certainly saved a lot of time now. There was a short pause, tense and defensive, and then the young man suddenly relaxed. He looked at me unsmilingly, but with something of an urchin's cheek.

'Somebody talking downstairs, I suppose. Mrs Broadbent, perhaps? She's got a foul mind, but she hits the nail on the head, as often as not.'

'Actually, my sergeant spotted it, and I imagine he's at this moment confirming it. He's right, then?'

'Oh yes, he's right. So what, anyway?'

His voice had taken on a slight cockney twang that was much more attractive and individual than the laundered neutrality of his usual speaking tones.

'Well, naturally,' I said, 'we think you probably know more about him than most. So far as we can see, he didn't have a wide circle of friends.'

'Don't I know it. The burden of being sole buddy and confidant was almost more than I could bear.'

'When did the relationship start?'

'Oh, six months ago, I suppose.'

'He seduced you?'

'Of course not. I seduced him.' The boy laughed for the first time, not attractively, but with an air of uncertainty showing through that proved he was still only a boy. 'It took time, I can tell you. I thought I was condemned to a lifetime of fatherly pattings, hand-squeezings and sentimental sighs. But finally I made it.'

'I presume you didn't go to all this trouble because you found Mr Brudenell attractive?'

'Too right. Who could? No doubt his old mother, of whom I have heard my fill over these last months. A whining old biddy she must have been, and no mistake. But for anybody else, he was a bit of a dead loss, though in a sort of way I did get fond of him, as one does.'

'What was it, then, you wanted from him? Did you get the job at the Palace with the aim of seducing him?'

'Good Lord, no. I knew nothing about him. And I'm

not particularly that way inclined. If I could have got the same out of the Princess, I'd have gone for her instead, and enjoyed myself a lot more. I could have had her, too, let me tell you. But she could never have been bothered to give me the help I needed, and in any case, she wouldn't have had the insight.'

'To do what?'

Malcolm Woodley paused. Then he lay back on his bed, his head pressed against the wall.

'I suppose it won't do any harm to say. I've never told anybody, except I suppose James, and him only by fits and starts, with hesitations and shy blushes. But him getting killed changes everything, doesn't it? Well—laugh away—I wanted to be a gentleman.'

'Oh,' was all I could think of to say.

'Yes, it's terribly Victorian, isn't it? The pushy young man trying to live up to his betters. We read *Great Expectations* at school. Most of the kids thought it a drag, but I didn't. I understood Pip. I didn't blame him a bit. I loved the middle bits where they taught him to behave, how to fit in. It said something to me, that book.'

'I don't think it said quite what the author intended.'

' 'Course it didn't. But books hardly ever do, do they? And anyway, he loaded the dice, by making Joe so good and forgiving and generous, so you were meant to feel Pip was a louse for wanting to get away from him. But what about if he hadn't had a Joe in the background? I certainly didn't. I just had my Mum.'

'Who was she?'

'Factory worker and part-time whore down the East End, Limehouse way. Foul-mouthed, didn't give a damn. I don't think she knew who my father was, but she always said it was a sailor off a Danish boat. Or Swedish, she was never quite sure. I don't think communication was too good, but it produced me. She called me Mel, by the way, on the birth certificate, after some American singer or other of the time. James made sure I changed it to Malcolm, so that got rid of about the only thing she ever gave me. I haven't set eyes on her since I left school.'

'You left home when you left school, did you?'

'Yes. First opportunity.'

'Why? To make it easier to become a gentleman?'

'Oh no, it wasn't as premeditated as that, at first. But I was working as a waiter, first in a scruffy Greek café, then in a rather good Italian restaurant in Soho. The pay was all right. But half the kids I'd known at school were out of work, and these days no one can say they're safe. So it came to me gradually that what I needed was a job that was a hundred per cent safe, where I could learn what I wanted to learn. I knew it would take time, I knew it would be like going back to school again. But I thought it was worth it. So I took a whacking drop in pay and came here. I've never regretted it.'

'So what precisely was it you wanted?'

'Oh God—how to explain? You know, when I was a waiter in that Italian restaurant, people used to come in—men—at lunch-time, doing business and that: smart, or well-dressed, anyway, public-school accents—ordering the right things, knowing about wine. Probably not out of the top drawer, otherwise they'd have been in a top-drawer restaurant, but still able to pass, When these men talked, half of what they said wasn't in the words: there was a sort of sign language underneath the words. They used it to signal to each other, and it showed they were of the same kind. Gentlemen. Natural rulers. People with a history. It made no difference that half of them probably had awful little jobs with PR firms. They were still part of the gentleman network. And that's what I wanted. I wanted to talk right, to dress right, to eat and drink right. Waiting showed me a door to this new world. I wanted to go through into it. I wanted to understand those signs.

Eventually, perhaps, to be able to make them myself. Do you blame me?'

I sighed. It seemed a sad little ambition.

'Of course not. But as you say, it does seem a bit out of date. Obviously you don't believe that Britain has become classless.'

Malcolm Woodley laughed. 'People who say that are always upper-middle or better themselves. The view from under the bridge is different.'

'And that was what you got from Brudenell?'

'Roughly. Of course, eventually I'd have gone on to someone with more finesse, someone more sophisticated, with better contacts. But he was good at all the obvious things: the food, and the clothes. That manner I have remote—you know—?'

'I know.'

'He taught me that. He said I had to learn not to give myself away before I could learn to relax again. And he was right. Without that . . . unapproachableness, I'd have made myself a laughing-stock a thousand times over.'

'Had he begun to introduce you round, then—I mean, get you into his set?'

'He didn't have a set. But we had put our toes into the water. It was hellish difficult. Say I'd gone to one of his little supper parties after the opera, or say we'd gone to the theatre together: the implications would have been totally obvious. And very damaging to James. Certainly one thing he could not afford to do was to "come out". So we had to be more subtle. If we went to the theatre we had to meet by chance in the bar at interval—then he could introduce me to anyone he knew. He could come to a restaurant knowing I'd be already sitting there—"Hello, old boy, fancy seeing you!" You know the drill. We must have had more stagey chance meetings than the couple in *Brief Encounter*. But it was beginning to work. I could pass. At first I had to stay very quiet; then I could start talking a bit. Soon I'll be able to take the initiative, make friends of my own.'

'You were beginning not to need him?'

'If you like to put it like that, though that certainly doesn't mean I wanted to get rid of him. But I knew where to buy clothes, and what to buy. I couldn't afford it, but then—few and good is the motto, isn't it? The eating and the drinking came easily. I'd picked up most of the drill, and James only had to teach me the philosophy behind the drill. When I've got a bit more confidence I'll start constructing a background for myself. Mum in Limehouse will not find a place in it. Well, that's it. That's my story, for what it's worth.'

'Right,' I said. 'That clears the air. Let's get down to the nitty-gritty, which is Mr James Brudenell.'

Malcolm Woodley sat up on the bed, and looked at me through cold, narrowed eyes.

'What about you coming clean first, then? You think it was murder, don't you?'

'If you mean the Police as a whole, we haven't made up our minds yet. If you mean me personally, yes, I do.'

'So do I,' said the boy frankly.

'Good. Now we both know what we're talking about. Why do you think that?'

'Well, first of all, from what we've heard downstairs, it was either suicide or murder. James was hardly the type to point a gun playfully at his head and then accidentally pull the trigger. James didn't live dangerously: he was a woolly vest and galoshes man. But the fact is, he wasn't the type to commit suicide either. He wouldn't have had the nerve. And anyway, he was perfectly happy. I don't suppose he'd ever been so happy in his life. He loved his job, and he loved me. There was no reason.'

'So things hadn't gone wrong between you?'

'Certainly they hadn't. As I say, I'd pretty soon have

been thinking of going on to someone else, but he definitely hadn't twigged that. You know, granted that he was a fussy, repressed little twit, he was really beginning to get a bit of enjoyment out of life. Now and again you'd have said he was a cat with two tails.'

'You wouldn't consider it possible that he was being blackmailed—for example, by someone else he had been involved with?'

'He hadn't been involved with anyone else. I was the first, I told you, and I was the only. Blackmail? It's a laugh. He would have told me.'

'You weren't blackmailing him yourself?'

'That's a stupid question. I wanted things from him, but money wasn't one of them. You say your sergeant noticed us: did he say it looked as if I was blackmailing him?'

'No, he didn't. And I don't think it looks like that. But in fact, I've always thought blackmail was a red herring. Now, when were you last together?'

'James and I? Just a couple of nights ago. Wednesday. I went to his flat. It wasn't something that happened very often. James was obsessed with the neighbours, though in fact it was a very shut-in place: nobody seemed to have much contact with anybody else. I hardly saw a soul, the times I went there.'

'Where did you meet, as a rule?'

'Mostly James came to my place. It's a room in Pimlico, and it was very much *infra* his *dig*, but he pretended he got a delicious sense of slumming it. Sometimes we drove out at weekends to one of the less popular country houses open to the public, or to a little-known restaurant. We once actually had a weekend in Brighton—off-season, separate rooms.'

'What did you do on Wednesday?'

'Nothing out of the ordinary. We usually began with what you might call tuition. That could take all shapes and forms. On Wednesday we talked about schools. James had lent me a book about public schools. We talked, and he told me the sort of things they don't put in books. The marks of a Winchester man, the special codes of a Harrovian. He had a bit of a complex about schools: he wished he'd gone to one of the major ones. Then we ate one of his ladylike little suppers, talked a bit, went to bed, and I went home about one o'clock.'

'What about his mood? Not depressed, or anything?'

'No, I tell you, he was happier these days than he'd ever been, I'd guess. In fact, he seemed a bit cock-of-the-walk about something or other.'

I groaned: 'Don't tell me—I can see it coming. The silly bugger didn't tell you what it was.'

'That's right.'

'All my cases are like that. Look, search your mind. Didn't he give you *any* indication?'

'Well, not really. I *presumed* it had something to do with his job here—at the Palace.'

'Why?'

'Because he didn't tell me anything about it. If anything happened to him (and not much did), he'd generally tell me all about it. But not if it was anything to do with the Princess. Or the Royal family in general. It wouldn't have done. Close as a clam he was. He called it "Proper Discretion". I once approached the subject of the Princess's love-life. Never again. He shut me up good and proper.'

'So he didn't say anything at all about why he was in a perky mood?'

'Perky doesn't quite describe it. He was, sort of indignant too—not outraged, but very tetchy. Not with me, but . . . with I don't know who.' He sat there in thought, trying to recreate the scene. 'When I got there I was completely whacked, and I said so. Only I called it utterly exhausted. We'd had a delegation in the afternoon of the Countrywoman's Guild of Needleworkers, and they'd stayed to tea, by arrangement, of course. Unbelievable, they were. Then the Princess had given a small dinner party, before going out to the theatre. That MP friend of hers was there, and I wouldn't mind betting she went on with him afterwards. Anyway, I said I was whacked, and James said he'd done a *very* good day's work (you know how he talked). I didn't ask what, because that was forbidden territory, but he did say, just after that, and quite out of the blue: "I do *hate* people who take *advantage*." And then: "People should realize I occupy a position of *trust*." '

'And that was all?'

'That was all I remember. We started in on the lesson then.'

'Tell me, when you were there, did you go into the study?'

'Oh yes. I always borrow an improving book from his collection.'

'Did you notice whether he had a big scrapbook open on the little table?'

Malcolm Woodley screwed up his eyes. 'Yes, it was there. It took up all the table. It's pretty pathetic, isn't it? He pasted in newspaper cuttings of the Princess, acres of them, just as though he was some besotted ageing Elvis fan.'

'Yes, I've looked at it. He didn't comment on the book on Wednesday?'

'No. He wouldn't. I think he was a bit embarrassed about it.'

We chewed the cud a bit more, but that in fact was about all I got out of young Woodley. By the end I felt he wasn't such an unendearing individual after all. I wondered what was to become of him. Gentlemen without money have one advantage over pseudo-gentlemen without money: they have contacts—family, schoolfellows, the old boy network. Probably Limehouse has pretty much the same sort of network. In fact, I believe that's the only way you can get work in the docks. But I did have an awful feeling that young Woodley was in danger of falling resoundingly between two stools.

I had a cosy chat with Joplin in the car, on the way back to the Yard. Mr Brudenell's little romance was of course no secret below stairs, but on this subject they could add nothing to young Woodley's own frank account. General opinion of the Princess was mixed. All the staff liked her, but a good half of them thought she needed a good smacking. 'She's a spoiled little minx,' the under cook had said, 'wilful and cunning as a fox, but she's only got to look at you, and smile, and she gets over your defences, and you smile back and do exactly what she wants.' As far as her boy-friends were concerned, three were known at the Palace. There had been an early, servile preference for the Honourable Edwin Frere, but this had soon effectively evaporated on closer acquaintance with the gentleman himself. The favourite was now Jeremy Styles, whose performances as Mr Darcy and Steerforth in television serials had apparently given him, in the eyes of the domestic staff, the patina of an honorary gentleman.

Oh well, perhaps there was hope yet for Young Woodley.

CHAPTER 11

High Places

By now Joplin and I both had 'doubles' at the Palace, policemen who could take over our security duties when necessary. However, next morning I had no alternative but to attend the Princess on an official function. She was visiting the Local Government Offices at Kilburn Town Hall, and since Kilburn contained a large Irish population, everyone was jittery. It seemed necessary for the senior man to be there. Even the lady-in-waiting came out of her upper-class carapace and expressed the opinion in the car that the Irish were 'lower than animals' – though since the only living thing I'd ever heard her express favourable opinions of were horses and dogs, this description didn't seem to me to have quite the cutting force she intended. Anyway, the local Irish apparently had other things on their minds that day than minor royalty, and apart from a boycott by some Labour councillors the visit went off very well, and we were back at Kensington Palace by half past twelve. It was an unexpectedly sunny early February day: daffodils were certainly not out, but there seemed to be daffodils in the air. I think the stirrings of spring affected the Princess too.

'Why,' she said, as we got out of the car, 'don't you have lunch with me?'

'I – er – '

'Oh *do*. I always have lunch with my security man at some time or other. Except McPhail. I didn't feel equal to that. But I do *love* policemen, you know, generally.'

'You remember I have another engagement for lunch, Your Royal Highness,' drawled Lady Dorothy, with warning and disapproval in the drawl.

'Quite, Dorothy,' said the Princess flatly. Thwarted, the lady-in-waiting trudged off towards the Palace. 'As if,' said the divine Helena, 'I'd think of sharing you.'

'Well, I – '

'Marvellous. Then we'll eat about one.'

And that's what we did, *tête-à-tête*. And I might as well tell you now, that is all we did, and (though Jan will never believe this) that was the closest I got to the Princess, alone, during the entire case. So this is not going to be one of those horribly vulgar books, usually written by Americans, where the reader is allowed to fulfil his dream fantasies by vicariously sleeping with royalty in the person of his hero. Not that I'm saying I couldn't have done, of course, if I'd gone all out.

Lunch was elegant nothings, beautifully served. Vol-au-venty things, you know what I mean, and some rather good sorbets. But lunch wasn't what it was all about. As I suspected, what the Princess really wanted was to pump me about James Brudenell's death, and as we toyed with our food (and the Princess managed to put away a considerable number of those elegant nothings, proving that she did not need to think about her figure, though throughout the meal I thought about it quite a lot) she put on a dazzling display of charm and low cunning to winkle information out of me. And I, for my part, put on the sort of plodding, straight-bat performance you get from an English eleven fighting for a draw against the West Indies. I won't burden you with that part of the conversation, because I told her nothing I haven't told you already, and withheld from her a great deal that I have. I think she found my discretion tiresome, though discretion was something she knew all about. At the end, however, she threw her own to the winds and came out with her personal preoccupations.

'Anyway, it's all a terrible bore, from my point of view, because I got the strongest possible warning from the Palace that for the next few days I was to lie as *low* as I possibly could. It's quite crushingly boring! The tedium of an evening on one's own. Last night I positively sat in front of that set watching Esther Rantzen talking about the labelling of detergents! Too horribly depressing. I nearly went against all my principles and rang up a friend.'

'Your principles, Ma'am?'

'That *they* have to call me. But then I remembered we'd have had to go to his flat, and I've already been there once this week, and that's another of my principles, so I stuck with the detergents. Have you noticed that if you say you'll go to their flat, they always *assume* things?'

'I can well imagine, Ma'am.'

'Do you know, I'm in *Private Eye* this week, which is lovely, but they go on about my "having the trousers off" someone I've never even met. To say that one has had the trousers off someone one hasn't had the trousers off is the worst injury one can do anyone, don't you agree? Besides, it's always the other way round. I've never had the exquisite pleasure of making love with someone reluctant.'

'I think it exceedingly unlikely you ever will, Ma'am.'

She giggled. 'Aren't we getting personal? Anyway, as I say, I was horribly good last night, in accordance with instructions from the Palace. Also, I'd made up my mind to be very virtuous for the next few days, because Daddy's coming.'

'Daddy? I mean, your father, Ma'am?'

'Yes. I do have one, you know.'

'I'm afraid I had rather assumed he was dead.'

'Oh no, he's not dead. He lives in Germany.'

'Yes, I knew he was German.'

'He's the Catholic Prince and Hereditary Elector of the State of Krackenburg-Hoffmansthal. The title goes back to the Holy Roman Empire. Do you know, I've never been really sure what the Holy Roman Empire was!'

'Nor have I, Ma'am,' I said truthfully. 'Except that someone said it was neither holy, nor Roman, nor an empire.'

'Well, that figures. Because my father is neither Catholic, nor Prince, nor an Elector. He's lapsed, there's no one to elect, and German titles were abolished years ago. They're only kept alive by the illustrated magazines.

Anyway, Daddy lives in this gloomy old castle not far from Munich, and I go and see him every summer—or I *say* I do, and I drop in on the way to somewhere more exciting. I mean, you can't actually *stay* there, because it's all ruined towers, gaping windows, draughty corridors and bats. You expect Count Dracula to come out at you any moment.' She giggled again. 'Though actually Daddy would fit the bill perfectly well, because he's tall and gaunt and gloomy, though terribly sexy too, and he's got a voice like a creaky door. I don't suppose he'd suck the blood of his own daughter, though, would he?'

'I'm sure he would have done so before now, if he'd felt the inclination,' I said gravely. 'So your father is coming to England, is he?'

'Yes—with this State Visit tomorrow. Of the Prince of Liechtenburg, who's his brother-in-law. He's been given an honorary court position and a place in the entourage, so though he's *persona* not particularly *grata* at the Palace, due to one or two things he said during the divorce, they're having to grit their teeth and bear it. Anyway, I'm going to be par*tic*ularly good during this visit, because no doubt there'll be a party or two to liven things up a bit. In fact, I know there will be, and one of them . . . well, you'll see. I suppose you'll be on duty?'

'Excuse me, Ma'am,' I said, with a mental shudder of anticipation, 'but you're not planning anything, are you?'

She gazed at me, wide-eyed.

'Good heavens, no. I don't *plan* things. And yet, all sorts of things seem to happen to me, I don't know why!'

'Wouldn't it be better, Ma'am, to settle down to a quiet life for a little?'

'Oh, much better,' she said, giggling. 'Only I just seem to attract danger, don't I? Actually, you're an awful hypocrite. Nobody goes into the Police for a quiet life. I bet you live *terribly* dangerously, and have millions of girl-friends, and have a real fizzing time when you're out of uniform.'

'Actually, Ma'am, I'm a particularly safe married man.'

'Oh—you're not *married*?'

'I'm afraid so, Ma'am. I am of age, you know.'

'Oh, I can see that. But what a waste. I'm always very careful about married men. I mean, the Press calls one marriage-breaker, and vamp, and things like that.'

'Mr Harry Bayle is a married man,' I said, greatly daring. 'And yet you go to his flat, Ma'am.'

'Oh, you *know*!' she said, still wide-eyed and giggly. 'That's who I was talking about earlier. Have you been trailing us, or something? In a trench-coat and trilby hat? I shall look out for you next time, and embarrass you in public. Actually, you know, Harry is as careful as if he was planning D-day or something, and with me being careful too, and the flat being *terribly* discreet, I really think we should be all right. I mean, I should hate to destroy his political career.'

'I'm sure he's unlikely to let anything come in the way of that, Ma'am.'

'Oh, do you think he's a go getter? An opp—opp—'

'Opportunist? Well, that's hardly for me to say, Ma'am.'

'I think he may be, you know. Because last time I was there in his flat, I found on the desk this speech of his, and it was all about mon—monetarism, and it was terribly in favour of the government's policies. I was ever so surprised. I think he must be going over. I do *hope* so, because it's so much *easier* with Tories, isn't it? I mean, people seem to expect it of them really, don't they?'

I neither asked her what 'it' was that was so much easier with Tories nor disillusioned her about the monetarist speech she had picked up. It was obvious somebody was not exercising the sort of care needed in the running of a cross-bench love-nest. One thing I could not see Mr Harry Bayle doing was changing his party: he must have been much too aware of the political fate of floor-crossers to do any such thing.

Anyway, I had to make my excuses now, because I had my appointment at Buckingham Palace. I didn't tell her that, though, and felt a bit of a louse going straight from lunching with her to a meeting designed to tie the silken chains more firmly around her. But I made my adieux with reasonable grace, and she opened those enormous grey 21-inch eyes, and said we must do it more *often*, and she wanted to know me so much *better*, and lots of things like that. I told myself that was the sort of thing she said to everybody—Birmingham Mayors, Comprehensive School Headmasters, Elders of the Church of Scotland. Still, the old heart missed a beat.

I don't think I'll tell you much about Buckingham Palace. It might contravene the Official Secrets Act, or something. It was all white and gold leaf, with pictures on the wall one had only read about, and it certainly didn't look as if the owner was having any trouble with the upkeep. Still, for all I know the back bedrooms may have been frightfully tatty. What I would like to have done was dawdle through gaping, like any old tourist, but in fact I was hurried along by a rather grander flunkey than Young Woodley (too old to be learning to be a gentleman, too self-assured to be anything other than what he so magnificently was), and finally I was closeted in a study the size of a provincial assembly hall in Jane Austen's time with the Secretarial Personage who had consented to the interview. He was probably only fourth or fifth in the secretarial pecking order, but he seemed pretty grand to me—lofty, languid and capable, like some nineteenth-century Foreign Secretary, someone who now and then condescended to come in off the grouse moors and solve the problems of Europe.

The Palace had been tactfully and briefly informed of the position vis-à-vis the Princess a couple of days before, when the Brudenell 'suicide' had come up. Naturally it (should that be 'It'?) was worried, and I took the opportunity to fill it in on all the details. It was clearly no good any longer holding back on them. The Secretarial Personage listened intelligently, but he stretched out his lean, epicene length as if he were listening to a fag excusing himself for burning the crumpets. At the end of the recital he sighed.

'Oh dear, oh dear. She does seem to have got herself involved with something, doesn't she?'

'Not necessarily she herself,' I pointed out loyally. 'She may be *threatened*, or else someone or other may have *involved* her.'

'You don't think,' said the Secretary wistfully, 'that it could have been Brudenell stepping out of line, and then committing suicide rather than face disgrace? We always wondered whether he was up to the job. And of course he was never *quite* the thing.'

Poor Brudenell. All that fussy snobbery, and then to be judged not quite the thing.

'The team investigating the death is pretty convinced it was not suicide,' I pointed out. 'No, as I see it, the possibilities are these. On the one hand, there may be some threat to the life of the Princess herself. This may have been what Snobby Driscoll intended to warn us about, and it may be the point of the Knightley episode— purely a case of mistaken identity. On the other hand, the Princess is by now pretty well known. Pictures of her all the time in the papers and the illustrated glossies.'

'Too true,' murmured the Secretarial Personage. 'It causes jealousy, I can tell you, among the older ladies.'

'I can imagine. Well, it's for that reason that I'm not altogether happy with the idea of the murderer (if one was involved there) making some kind of mistake. And if the Knightley business was mistaken identity, it's not easy to account for the death of Brudenell.'

'No. I can see that. And the other possibility?'

'That in some way or other the Princess Helena is involved in some kind of criminal conspiracy. Quite unwittingly, of course—against her will, without her knowledge.'

'Quite,' breathed the Personage.

'The fact that Snobby Driscoll knew of it suggests the involvement of some crook of the usual type at some stage of the conspiracy. In other words, not the type of person that the Princess would normally associate with.'

'But she associates with such assorted types,' put in the Secretary plaintively.

'Quite,' I breathed, in imitation. 'But as far as I know, no one hitherto of the criminal classes. In any case, whichever of the explanations is the true one, one is worried for the Princess. Either her life or her reputation is at risk. Which is why we have tried to be quiet and tactful about the whole business.'

'Greatly appreciated—' drawled the Secretary.

'And in fact we have said nothing to the Princess herself. Since we feel, on the whole—'

'That she is not to be trusted,' supplied the Personage coolly.

'In this particular matter,' I insisted. 'Not to keep quiet about it. She seems to court excitement. If we had told her, she might well have told one of her . . . well, boy-friends. Who might, in turn, have been involved. The problem is, we have no desire to restrict Her Royal Highness's private life. She's young, she does an awful lot of very dreary jobs—'

'We don't admit that here,' breathed the Secretary. 'She does her public duties, you know.'

'Still, all those old people's homes and geriatric units,' I persisted. 'It can't be much fun for a bright young thing like her to specialize in the old.'

'We don't *specialize*,' rebuked the Secretary. 'You make it sound like some kind of character actor. I'll have a word with Brudenell's successor if she's been overdoing it in that direction.'

'Ah yes, Brudenell's successor. Now, I wanted to say something about that. It seems to me—and no doubt it's occurred to you too—that some very definite qualities are required in him.'

The Secretarial Personage sighed.

'We know, we know. We've talked about it, up to the Very Highest Level. She's an artful little minx, strictly off the record. And she enjoys her—what shall we say?—conquests. We knew this all along, of course. Impregnability to her charms seemed the first requirement when we appointed Brudenell.'

'Possibly you went a little too far in that direction,' I murmured.

'Quite . . . *Quite* . . . And of course, he was terribly well-meaning, and loyal, and discretion itself, which is vital . . . but perhaps not really *strong* enough.'

'Quite,' I murmured. 'I suppose there is no question of her father, at times, providing the restraining influence required?'

The Secretary, literally, and with more energy than he had displayed hitherto, shuddered.

'No. *No*. Dreadful heredity there, you know. He's got a mixture of German melancholy with quite obsessively rampant sexuality. His mother was a Bourbon Parma. No, he most definitely would not provide the restraining influence you are talking about.'

'Well,' I said, sticking to my guns, 'you will need someone, in my opinion, who will take a firm line with her, and stick to it. Who won't stand any nonsense. Someone willing to wield the big stick if necessary.'

'Ye-e-es,' said the Secretarial Personage. 'Strong-minded, determined, impervious to feminine charms. There *is* such a person.'

'Good.'

'Only she happens at the moment to be Prime Minister,' he said, with a wistful sigh.

CHAPTER 12

Acting Styles

When I got back to Scotland Yard after my glimpse of life at the top, I found myself in the middle of a conference about security during the State Visit, due to start next day. Not the routine safety on the streets during the drive through London and the various public festivities, but security during the rather more private events, including a gala performance at Covent Garden and a dinner given for the Queen at the Savoy by the Prince of Liechtenburg. All this sort of stuff was vital but dull, and I won't bore you with the details. This is not one of those police procedural books, where you get so much detail about all the routine slog involved in crime that you wear out the soles of your shoes just reading them.

After the conference was over I could go to my office and catch up with the details of the Brudenell murder, as they were emerging from the painstaking investigations of the dour McPhail. The report on the gun was the first thing I looked at. It had almost certainly been bought in the States. Of course (granted their laws) there was no record of where it had been obtained, or who by, but from the number it seemed likely that it had been sold in the first half of the previous year. The Princess had paid a visit to the United States that March, where she had received an honorary degree from a little-known New England university, and attended the opening night of the Royal Ballet season in Philadelphia. Mr James Brudenell had accompanied her. It seemed, therefore, as if he was indeed shot with his own gun, probably bought to protect himself against the murderous marauding muggers and crackpots who (in British mythology) make up fifty per cent of the American population.

Another report lying on my desk confirmed (by analysing dust samples) that it was the most recent of Brudenell's scrapbooks that had lain open on his study table on the day before he died, though all the scrapbooks had been fairly recently consulted. The report was unable to suggest any particular pages that had been of interest to him. He seemed, in fact, to have worked his way methodically through it. McPhail had left the scrapbook in question in my office, and I conscientiously went through it too. It was the fullest possible record of the Princess's activities from day to day, with the announcement from the Court Circular heading the page, and with reports and press photographs underneath, sometimes from local newspapers, more often from national ones. I struggled through the unveilings of statues, the launchings of gun-boats, the charitable annual general meetings, the visits to geriatric units, but the book said nothing to me. What I was really looking for was a mention of the five places on Bill Tredgold's list, but beyond a visit to Keswick, in Cumberland, to open a Youth Hostel I could find none, not even during the engagements in the Midlands one weekend the previous November, when I presumed she had first made Bill Tredgold's acquaintance. It was all a big disappointment. It seemed likely the scrapbook was of no significance at all.

There was also a report on the typewriter, and it was just as I expected. The only fingerprints on it were

Brudenell's, but all the letters which appeared in the second half of the typed note had little smudges on the edges of the keys, while the 'j', for example, which was only used for the 'John' in the opening, had no such mark. It was this report which made it quite clear we were dealing with murder. The killer had not been quite clever enough.

I also had waiting for me on my desk a rather negative report from the police at Shrewsbury. They had found out that four of the addresses in the guest book at The Wrekin, Knightley, were phoney or questionable. Two 'married couples' had given false addresses (which was not surprising), but so had one single man and one woman. The woman's was in handwriting so indecipherable that it was possible there was no intention to deceive. On the subject of the wine and the glasses they had drawn a blank. They had visited all the off-licenses and pubs, and very generously were going now to continue with the classier establishments in the Shrewsbury area—the three-star hotels, the clubs, the better restaurants. They did not hold out much hope.

So there it was—the routine grinding ahead, turning out little driblets of results. Though we were now sure that we were investigating a murder, and probably two murders, the advances otherwise could not be said to be encouraging. And meanwhile I was faced next day with a spectacular interruption in the form of a State Visit. Normally at this point I would have gone back to the flat and soothed the nerves by chatting over the case with Jan, and parrying all her questions about the interior of Buckingham Palace. But Jan and Daniel had driven back to Newcastle the day before, slightly late for the beginning of Spring term, and the best the flat could offer me was a bath and an evening's television. I felt a bit like the Princess—starved of glamour and high life. That sort of thing can act like a drug, I suppose. Luckily a shot of the necessary was to hand. I remembered the invitation I'd had from Jeremy Styles. It was an hour to curtain up at the St George's theatre. It was the first time I'd ever dropped in on an actor in his dressing-room. Routine-bound a policeman's lot may be, but now and again you do see life!

I just sent my name in at the stage door, but it acted like a charm, and in a matter of minutes I was being led through dark, linoed corridors (theatrical glamour seems to end at the footlights) to the star's dressing-room.

'Ah, my friend the cop,' said Jeremy Styles. 'Sit there and talk to me while I make up, and I'll study you for when I star in a Francis Durbridge.'

'You wouldn't play the cop,' I said. 'You'd play the cocktail-drinking commuter-belt lady-killer.'

'What a word to use. Not a Freudian slip, I hope.'

I sat down quite happily and looked around me. Jeremy Styles was half-dressed for the part, and making up his face with a rather grubby towel round his shoulder to protect his shirt. He dabbed, and drew lines, and studied the result with a total professional expertise. He was ministered to and fussed over by his dresser, a small, tough, elderly man. I suppose the theatre is the last place where you find the total domestic devotion that in an earlier age all the great families would demand from their servants. Even fifty years ago, a great lady might expect to have an elderly, grim-faced personal maid, the female equivalent of this dresser, a woman whose devotion was total, who chivvied while she curtsied, grumbled while she ministered, who had been with the lady since girlhood, knew her infinitely better than her husband did, and made the lives of the other servants hell by insisting on her special relationship. I guessed that Jeremy Styles's dresser was of this sort: perhaps he had been inherited from his father or mother. It was quite clear, anyway, that there was nothing that Styles would not say in his presence: he treated him, in fact, as if he were not there, though he would probably have created hell if he were not. I was reminded of the old story of Queen Victoria and the Empress Eugenie in their box at the opera: Eugenie looked round for her chair before she sat down. Victoria sat down knowing her chair would be there. Jeremy Styles came from an acting dynasty.

'And how go your investigations?' asked Styles, slapping and patting his cheeks like a love-besotted masseur. 'Do I gather you have a corpse on your hands?'

'Yes. I do.'

'Careless.'

'And do I gather you have been talking to the Princess?'

'Of course. We talk almost every day. Especially now, when I gather they're keeping her on a fairly tight rein.'

'If,' I said, 'she is allowing herself to be kept.'

'I expect Lady Dorothy, the upper-crust policewoman, is doing her best. It's what she's there for.'

'She's not an old friend of the Princess's, then?'

'Good Lord, no. Can you imagine it? She was picked because she was utterly repressed and respectable, and a sort of throw-back to old Queen Mary's time. And Helena accepted her because she's fairly repellent physically, and as you've probably noticed Helena is a vain little thing, and thought the piquant contrast would be all to the good. I think it works out very well. Lady Dorothy has someone during the day to whom she can drone on endlessly about her family tree and her noble relatives—she's a sort of walking stud-book, as you've probably found out. To the point of obsession. And in the evenings Helena is left free to do what she wants, to go to places Lady Dorothy wouldn't be seen poking the sharp end of her Roman nose inside the door of.'

'I know,' I sighed. 'If only she wouldn't—'

'Go to that sort of place? Give up the idea. She's never going to grow up, you know. How could she, in that sort of environment, doing that sort of job practically from her teens?'

'You once said all actors were fourteen,' I said. 'I suppose that applies to Royals as well.'

'Exactly. The environments are practically identical: the hothouse atmosphere, the public adulation, the little "in" group, with in-fighting and in-loving, the imprisonment of being a known face, being constantly in the public eye. The only chance for Helena would be to marry a rather dull man, and sink into respectable obscurity.'

'I can't imagine it happening,' I said.

'Nor can I. You realize she hasn't got a brain in her head?'

'No-o-o,' I said, a bit dubiously. 'I remember using that phrase myself once. And yet, the more one sees her . . .'

'She's got cunning. Not brains. She has the sort of imagination needed to get what she wants. At least she's the sort of egotist who understands other people. The egotists who don't are the sad, the unsuccessful ones. And because she understands them, she knows how to use them. But she hasn't got brains. You take her to a play and listen to her comments afterwards. They wouldn't do credit to a ten-year-old. I think she just sits there planning what she'll wear tomorrow. She's totally self-absorbed. That's what I love about her. I understand it. She's an actress.'

'The trouble is,' I said, 'that her life isn't as exciting as a real acting life would be.'

'You have illusions about the stage,' said Jeremy Styles. 'The reason actresses like scenes—and actors too now and then—the reason they throw tantrums, is because their lives are so confoundedly dull that they wouldn't be bearable otherwise. Dreary rehearsals, dreary dressing-rooms, dreary repetitions of the same old motions night after night, like being on the production line of a factory.

It's the same with Helena. Her life is one long crushing boredom. She phoned me, you know, to get me along to the Wellington Club that night. That's typical. Just now and then she has to light a firework and watch the sparkles.'

'I'm very much afraid,' I said, 'that she's planning to send up a rocket in the near future.'

'Of course she is,' said Styles. 'And I wouldn't mind betting when it is.'

'Oh?'

He took one more look at his face, then took off the towel, let it drop to the floor, and while his dresser retrieved it began setting his costume to rights. Then he went over to a little shelf in the corner and took from it a card.

'An invitation,' he said, gazing at it with mock awe, 'from Edwina, Lady Glencoe.'

'That name rings a bell.'

'A bell the size of Great Tom, I should think,' said Jeremy Styles. 'She was notorious in her time. She wore out so many lovers in her youth she made the original Glencoe massacre look like a minor mopping-up operation. Now she's just a fairly disreputable old bag. Now why should she invite me to a party?'

'Because she has designs on you?'

'That, I admit, is one interpretation. It is, however, a rather special party. Lady Glencoe is a director of Covent Garden, thanks to her entire and utter ignorance of things operatic. The party is to be held in the Crush Bar tomorrow night. After the Gala Performance—'

'In honour of the State Visit of His Highness the reigning Prince of Liechtenburg.'

'Precisely. Now, beyond having once understudied the apprentice in *Peter Grimes*, I have no connection with Covent Garden. Nor have I the slightest connection with

Edwina, Lady Glencoe. What's the betting I've been invited—'

'At the behest of the Princess Helena.'

'Exactly. And what's the betting that Edwin Frere has also been invited. And her MP boy-friend. And even her old flame in the world of football—have you got to meet him yet?'

'Not yet.'

'A real charmer. He's a Northern Irelander. A Protestant. He has all the quiet modesty and delicate tact we know so well from their political leaders. Well now, if I'm right, that should be quite a line-up.'

'Plus, I shouldn't mind betting,' I added gloomily, 'the young lady's father.'

'Ah, the blood-sucking Bavarian. Very likely. All the chemical ingredients for a really nasty blow-up. In other words, the little scene at the Wellington last week whetted the Princess's appetite for confrontation politics. She is thirsty for men fighting over her, and she plans something on a more extended scale.'

'Will you go?'

'Oh, I'll go. But I certainly won't make a scene, or play up if anyone else makes one. In fact, much though I love her, I have the fancy to disappoint the young Helena. She's getting just that bit too spoilt by success. But if she's to be disappointed, I need co-operation. I'm quite sure the last thing Harry Bayle would want would be a public fracas. On the other hand, one can hardly expect the same of Edwin Frere. Or the footballer. That one thrives on being sent off the field. So we shall have to see. Perhaps you could do something about it?'

'I doubt it,' I said. 'I suppose I could try.'

'Blessed are the peacemakers,' said Jeremy Styles.

'But who these days would want to inherit the earth?'

'That,' said Styles, 'is the meek.'

'Thank God. I'm safe then,' I said.

But I was so disturbed by the prospect of tomorrow evening that I forgot to ask Jeremy Styles to keep me posted about his dates with the Princess. In the event, it didn't matter. In a couple of days the case was solved, and I was able to stop playing Paul Pry into other people's love-lives. I was beginning to feel like I did in my early days on the beat, shining my torch into the back seats of cars.

Anyway I watched a bit of Jeremy Styles's play from the back of the stalls—it was quite funny, but I much prefer the sort of play where you can hope for some minor character to pop in and say 'Anyone for tennis?' One prolonged singles match does get tiring. So I went home and heated up something from the deep freezer, and then I rang Jan in Newcastle (she has the sort of digs with a phone in the hall) and I brought her up to date on the developments in the case, which added a hefty sum to my telephone bill. She in her turn gave me some details (she's good at that sort of thing) about the past life of Edwina, Lady Glencoe.

'You can't say you aren't mixing in the best circles,' she said.

'Highest, perhaps,' I countered. 'High as well-hung pheasant.'

'You're just an inverted snob. I bet before you go to bed you'll go and look them all up in Debrett, and *drool* over the company you'll be keeping.'

I didn't, in fact. Actually I went straight to bed, to sleep fitfully and drowse dreadingly on the subject of tomorrow's State Visit. Jan, later on, was the first to point out that it would have been very much better if I had done what she had foretold.

CHAPTER 13

State Visit

The Principality of Liechtenburg consists of ten or twelve square miles of Disneyland buildings perched on the edge of some crag in the middle of the Alps, ruled over by a monarch who adds new shades of diminution to the word 'princeling'. It is the sort of state fit to have an American musical made out of it, and not much else. The present Prince's ancestors had so skilfully played off Austria against France, and both against Switzerland, that he had been allowed to keep his little pocket-handkerchief of edelweiss-bespattered rock, and in the twentieth century it had become a fictitious place of residence for the beautiful people, an accommodation address for the tax-dodging businessman, a sort of numbered bank-box to the world. In the normal course of events the Prince of vaguely ridiculous little states like Liechtenburg would hardly be in line for the honour of a State Visit. These days, however, Liechtenburg seemed to correspond cosily with Britain's vision of itself. So here were the Prince and the Princess, with three of their children, their Hofmeister, their Prime Minister and Foreign Minister, and seven or eight regular or specially appointed members of their court. As some wit said, the streets of Liechtenburg must suddenly have seemed very empty.

The Prince of Liechtenburg (which is a landlocked state) nevertheless had a yacht, stationed at Nice, which was nominally the Liechtenburg Navy. This yacht was commanded by an Admiral (who in the winter months doubled as Master of the Horse), and the Admiral sailed the yacht from Nice to Harwich at the commencement of the State Visit. At Harwich the Prince and his entourage were welcomed on behalf of the Queen by one of her cousins, who transferred the party into the Royal Train and accompanied them to Liverpool Street Station. Here they were to be met by the Queen and all sorts of royal and governmental personages, and thence the visitors would take their places in the carriage procession which would make its way through the narrow streets around the station (which only needed that to make them impossible), and eventually into the Strand for the triumphal drive through central London, along streets thronged with early tourists (continentals still under the impression that Britain was cheap), and thence to the safety of Buckingham Palace.

The security during the procession was not, thank Heaven, my affair. I was merely to wait in the vicinity of the Princess Helena at Liverpool Street Station, and then go off duty until the Gala.

So there we all were, assembled under the grimy arches of that least welcoming of railway stations. How shall I describe the glittering scene for you? How shall I describe the glittering scene without lapsing into BBC commentator's prose? I think, if you don't mind, I'll give it a big miss. Can we take it that the Queen was looking regal in a turquoise shantung something or other, that the Duke was looking gallant and handsome in the uniform of the 42nd Lancers, and the Prince of Wales was looking fairly gallant and fairly handsome in the uniform of the Third Welsh Borderers, and the Princess of Wales was looking absolutely yummy? Oh, and the Queen Mum was looking as usual in one of those feathery hats and pale blue outfits of the kind she's been wearing since the days when she called on Snobby Driscoll's mum, and which as a matter of fact I rather like?

Let's skip all that stuff, and just say that the Prince of Liechtenburg (a grey-haired, rather distinguished, scholarly-looking man) alighted from the train, was welcomed, and walked through the station with the Queen to take his place in the first carriage. After that, all went according to Protocol: the Princess of Liechtenburg (who looked as if she might be a dab hand with an apfel strudel) paired off with the Duke, and so on down to my little Helena, who rode in the sixth carriage with the second son of the Liechtenburg Prince—a boy of fourteen whom it was no doubt thought she would be safe with, though in situations less overwhelmingly public I'm not so sure.

But before she got to her coach the Princess Helena had one other duty to perform. Alighting from the train just ahead of the Court and governmental personnel, presumably in some sort of honorary position that was neither fish nor fowl, was her father, and the Princess left her teenage Prince for a moment and went to hug her progenitor. The gesture was not, I suspected, sincere, but she did it sincerely. Cameras clicked. Then she made her way demurely through the station to her carriage, as usual arousing a very special (vaguely lecherous) cheer.

My duty was over. I lingered behind and took a better look at her father, Prince Rupert of Krackenburg-Hoffmansthal: he was indeed tall and melancholy—with, at first glance, the look of a poet or a musician, a somewhat troubled look, as if plagued by *Angst* or constipation. Then one saw the full lips and the roving eye, and realized he had another side to his nature—less a Werther than Werther's contemporaries, the sons of George III.

'Off course I haff been here before,' I heard him say to the Buckingham Palace equerry, in that remarkably harsh and unattractive voice that the Princess had mentioned to me. 'I voss here many time viss my late vife. Yes, indid. London holds many unhappy memories for me!'

He laughed a hollow laugh, like the scraping together of rusty knives, and disappeared through the station arches to the waiting world outside.

Me, I got into a police car and made my way through all the cordoned-off side streets, and three-quarters of an hour later was standing outside Buckingham Palace as the carriage procession arrived, in a Mall moderately thronged with observers—for even minuscule royalty gets a better turn-out than important Presidents. One by one the carriages, with their waving figures like models in mechanical clocks, turned into the Palace. The Princess Helena was talking animatedly to her young Prince, who was obviously planning to marry her when he got older. She nevertheless kept up her quota of waves, and even gave a special one for me when she saw me by the gates. The old heart missed a beat again. Clever girl. Then the coach disappeared round the side of the Palace, and I knew she was safely cocooned in all that plush and gilt until it was time to go to the Gala.

Normally the first evening of a State Visit would have been devoted to a State Banquet. But that evening was the only one on which Covent Garden could produce a suitable gala opera, and since the Prince had especially expressed the wish to see an opera (and the Queen had had perforce to grit her teeth and bear it), the banquet had been postponed to the second day. The Prince had spent his young manhood in post-war Vienna, had worshipped at the feet of Ljuba Welitsch, Lisa Della Casa, Hilde Gueden. Liechtenburg did not run to an Opera, though it did have a cinema show on Wednesdays and Saturdays. The opera was to be Meyerbeer's *L'Africaine*—hardly the obvious choice, since it is one aria surrounded by five acts of padding and lots of pretty scenery, but it happened to be what the Royal Opera were performing at the time.

So I spent the afternoon at Covent Garden,

familiarizing myself with the place and the security arrangements. I had been there before, of course, but of late years only in the upper reaches, and that seldom. The Royal party was to occupy the central section of the Grand Tier, where they could both see and be seen. At interval they were to go to the private room behind the Royal Box, where they would mingle with the Covent Garden top brass. No possible danger there. Operatic people get more than enough sublimation for their violent impulses. The security arrangements at the Garden were supervised by the Palace, and they were, of course, impeccable. After I had got the lie of the land in that part of the house, I asked about the arrangements for Lady Glencoe's party. The official whom I questioned seemed to be suppressing with difficulty raised eyebrows and lewd innuendoes. He pointed out to me three boxes where Lady Glencoe's intimate party would sit. After the performance they would go back to the Crush Bar, where they would be joined by the rest of the invitees, by the directors and by the odd critic and performer, for this was an official House party. Most of those attending would have been sitting in other parts of the house, or in some cases (Jeremy Styles, for example), would not have attended the opera at all.

'Does she have this sort of party often?' I asked.

'Not infrequently,' sniffed the functionary. 'After the House's more social evenings, as a rule. She is on the Board to help with such things: the social side is considered important, and Lady Glencoe is very good at gathering . . . notables.'

'So that's why she's on the Board?'

'Yes. The workings of the Board are as mysterious as those of the Masons. Lady Glencoe is rumoured to be tone-deaf, which must make the evenings she is forced to spend here a considerable trial to her.'

'Would you have a list of her personal guests tonight?'

'Naturally. We wouldn't let just anyone into those areas of the House. Would you like to see it?'

The list, of course, confirmed the suspicions of Jeremy Styles, who obviously knew his Helena very well indeed. Invited by Lady Glencoe herself to the after-the-performance party were Henry Bayle, MP, the Honourable Edwin Montague Frere, and Mr James McAphee (better known as Jimmy), whose name I recognized as that of a roustabout Charlton Athletic player whose reputation for violence and foul language rivalled that of your average English supporter. Also gracing the occasion would be Prince Rupert of Krackenburg-Hoffmansthal, and of course the Princess Helena herself.

Well, forewarned is forearmed. There was one thing I could do, and I did it: I rang up McAphee and made it clear to him that if there were any trouble at the party I would not only arrest him, but also oppose bail, and he would be out of the Cup qualifying game on Saturday. I won't burden you with what he said to me, which is the sort of thing that gets books banned in Home Counties libraries, but I'm no mean hand at that sort of thing myself too, and in the end we came to some sort of unamicable agreement.

So there we were, all prepared. At half past six I was in attendance at Kensington Palace, and the journey to the Opera House was uneventful. The Royals arrived one by one, and gathered in the room behind the Royal Box. At five to seven the Queen and the Duke and the Prince and Princess arrived, and at seven (Meyerbeer provides an awfully long evening's music) the Royal party took their places. This time it was quite literally a glittering occasion: you've never in your life seen so many diamond tiaras, shimmering dresses, bosoms weighed down with the family emeralds, portly chests sporting decorations for services in the field or in Whitehall. The opera definitely took second place as spectacle to what was to be witnessed in the front of the house. I suspected that ninety per cent of those there wouldn't, in fact, have been able to tell *Tristan* from *The Tales of Hoffmann*, but they certainly woke up and became lively at interval.

I won't burden you with details of the performance. I stood at the back of the dress circle and watched bits of it, and the story made *The Pirates of Penzance* look like a masterpiece of realistic theatre. The music had stirring bits, jolly bits and totally ludicrous bits. The Queen succeeded in looking interested. She did not succeed in looking as if she were enjoying herself. The audience was more interested in what was going on in the Grand Tier than in what was going on on stage. At interval, as I said, the Royals did not go into the Crush Bar to mingle with *hoi polloi* (though that is hardly the most apt description, since tickets sold for about £25 a pop), but went instead to the private room, and chatted with the operatic bigwigs. I attended them in my security capacity—there was nothing to fear there, but lots to overhear. The Princess talked to the Prince of Liechtenburg's eldest son, on whom she seemed to be having an effect even more striking than that on his younger brother. I had read my evening papers. They were speculating (undeterred by the fact that the two had never clapped eyes on each other before today) on a romance between the pair. I was quite sure that Helena had read her evening papers too. This was the sort of speculation she fed on, greedily, unashamedly, and which in her turn she liked to feed.

I managed to get close to Prince Rupert, bending his height proprietorially over a rather delicious specimen of our minor royals. He looked like a stork waiting to gobble a tasty morsel of sea-food. Funny how eating and drinking images seemed to cluster around Helena's father. Perhaps Helena's mother felt she had been sucked dry and then cast off. Prince Rupert was saying:

'Helena, off course, takes after me. That is something they could not rob me off. She hass a romantic nature, a poetic soul. She stands out against theess bourgeois, mercantile soulss. You too, my dear, haff a romantic soul. I can see it . . .'

It was all too Franz Lehar for words. I could see the delectable lady (recently married into this bourgeois, mercantile family) cast a nervous glance in the direction of her husband.

As they all trouped back for the second act, I heard a Very Distinguished Lady Indeed remark to Her Husband that so far it wasn't as bad as she'd expected—a judgement she probably had to revise drastically before the end of a very long evening.

But end it did, eventually. The audience applauded dutifully (it made more sense when, after the lights went up, they applauded the royal party). There was one royal duty to be gone through before the evening was over: most of the occupants of the royal box went backstage to shake hands with the performers, dutifully lined up, paws at the ready. The press got some splendid photographs, including one of Prince Rupert gazing ravenously down into the cleavage of the buxom black mezzo who had sung Sélinka. It made a very good cover for the next issue of *Private Eye*. At last all the official stuff was over, and the royal party could slope off home for a cup of cocoa and some well-earned shut-eye (I imagined them all curled up around their hotties, superlative, royal hotties stamped with a monogram—corgi rampant against a gules background).

Me, I had left Joplin to look after the Princess in the last minutes, and had slipped into a greasepainty loo, where I had changed into a dinner-jacket. Then, some way behind the Princess, and leaving Joplin on guard in the corridors, I went back into the front of house and towards the Crush Bar, my valley of Glencoe, with something of the same emotions that Miss Blandish must have had when she entered the hideout of the Grisson gang.

CHAPTER 14

Lions' Den

In the plushy grandeur of the Crush Bar, in an area roped off specially for the occasion, the party was already in full swing. The arrival of the Princess Helena had created the expected stir, with the usual accompaniment of gush and fawn. By the time I got to the top of the stairs she was already the centre of an admiring group, which included Harry Bayle—taking time off from egalitarian politics, and looking, in his tuxedo, holding his cut-glass tumbler of Scotch, every inch the Establishment's choice of future Prime Minister. The Princess smiled, ogled, giggled discreetly and was somehow regally provocative, and in all these ways she contrived to raise the sexual temperature in the room. Which, apart from those guests who were directly attributable to her, was not high.

I had hoped to be able to slip in unnoticed and go about my business of doing all in my power to avert Helena's intentions to create well-orchestrated brouhaha. But it was not to be. As I entered the roped-off area I was hailed by a fruity, gin-laden voice.

'Perry Trethowan, isn't it? *How* good of you to come. I knew your Uncle Lawrence, you know. And your mother. I'm *dying* to have a talk with you, dear man . . .'

And here I was being commandeered by a strawberry-coloured woman, showing an unsuitable amount of puffy shoulder, who seemed to be assuming rights of property over me. Who could it be but Edwina, Lady Glencoe?

I had gathered by now the basic facts about Lady Glencoe. Nothing in her life had been particularly secret. She had had her first taste of notoriety in her debutante year, when she had followed the example of Nancy Cunard and taken a Negro pianist as her lover. So popular were Negro pianists at that time that there were not enough of them to go round, and I have the impression that boatloads of them must have been shipped over from the States, with Society Ladies standing on the wharf at Southampton and making bids. It was one way out of the Depression, I suppose. Because this was the early 'thirties, when the Prince was dancing with Wallis at the Embassy Club and the Labour Government was trying to reduce the dole from seventeen shillings.

When Negro pianists went out, the lady had taken a succession of lovers—energetic peers of the realm, a left-wing poet waiting to be killed in Spain, an Indian patriot in exile, a chargé d'affaires at the German Embassy, and a Welsh boxer. She had driven an ambulance for both sides in the Spanish Civil War, until they begged her not to. She had run a hostel for exiled Poles in the war, and later extended her charity to exiled Frenchmen, Belgians, Norwegians and Czechs. At the end of the war she was decorated, with an ambiguously worded citation. By then she was Lady Glencoe, and had produced an heir for the uncouth laird who had been hypnotized by her already matured charms. By the hard winter of 1947 he had hurled her out into the snow, he to go on to other Lady Glencoes, she to become hostess to the less hidebound younger lights of the Conservative Party. She claimed all the credit for making Macmillan Prime Minister, and played a walk-on part of a discreditable nature during the Profumo affair. Now, when the party had fallen into the hands of grocers and grocers' daughters, she was a spent force, reduced to charity do's and operatic gaieties. But she carried herself with the air of one who had done a thing or two in her time, and might tell all, if only the Sunday papers would up their miserable offer for her life story.

'Lady Glencoe?' I said nervously, because the figure, like a barrel of wobbly lard, was wobbling uncomfortably close to my midriff. 'Yes, I'm Perry Trethowan. I don't know how you know me. I'm only here in my official capacity.'

'But darling! I won't let you blush like a rose unseen, or whatever flower it is. You're so famous! Your picture in all the papers! So jealous-making! At the time I *marked you down*, so let's have no *shrinking*. I knew you the moment you came up the stairs. And Dorothy confirmed it.'

I cast a look of ingratitude in the direction of the lady-in-waiting, who was chatting to a feeble-looking relative with a receding hairline and chin to match.

'You'll have a Scotch. Waiter! Here!'

'I'll just hold one—'

'No, drink plenty, dear boy. It's on the house. In these dreadful times that's the only way to drink really sufficiently. Oh, there's darling Davina. I must fly. But I expect you to stay to the end, so that we can have a *gorgeous* chat over the dregs about your daddy's going. Have fun, darling!'

Oh dear. Ripeness is all, said the poet, and I confess I could have dumped Lady Glencoe and all her dated daring on to the poet without a moment's regret. She certainly wasn't what I would have chosen for a *tête-à-tête* at the end of a long and tiring day. But with a bit of luck it might be avoided. I made for a quiet oasis where I might inconspicuously see and hear.

'You do get around, don't you?' said an unpleasant voice in my ear, as I was sliding my bulk through the throng to a corner which hadn't got singers or critics or upper-class nincompoops cluttering it up. I turned round into the vapid, discontented face of the Honourable Edwin Frere.

'Oh well,' I said, with hastily assumed bonhomie, 'I try to live it up while I'm here, you know.'

'Don't give me all that stuff about being just back from the colonies. I know who you are. You're what I believe is nowadays called the fuzz. I should have guessed by your size. I don't know what you were doing at the Wellington the other night . . .'

'We're entitled to our moments of relaxation, you know.'

'Hmmm. Well, it seems odd. Because you couldn't have known I was going to invite the Princess. I suppose you're guarding her tonight?'

'Something of the sort,' I agreed.

'Pity you don't try guarding her from some of the types she encourages.' We had come to rest in a corner near the bar, and he surveyed the room with undisguised contempt.

'Look at them. That little actor fellow I gave his come-uppance to. What a jerk! That MP she's always going about with. He's an out-and-out Communist, you know, though you wouldn't think it to look at him. And look at that one over there: he's a footballer. My God, just imagine—a footballer mixing with this mob. As far as I'm concerned, they're really off types, the lot of them. I've half a mind to tell her so.'

'You'd be a fool to,' I said. He looked at me bellicosely. 'Can't you see, you're the one with all the cards. However she may play around now, you're the only one that's remotely acceptable. Can you see her walking down the aisle with a Northern Ireland footballer?'

'Who said anything about marriage?' muttered Edwin Frere, but I could see the idea wasn't a new one to him.

'You've only got to sit still and be a good boy, and the apple will drop into your lap,' I went on.

'It beats me why all these jerks are here, then,' he said, after thinking it over.

'Well, it's obvious: the Princess likes a bit of excitement – you've seen that yourself. Then, when she's been stirring the pot for some time, it boils over – and the Princess slips out, leaving someone else to pick up the pieces and shoulder the blame. She's a past mistress of self-preservation. That's why you're all here tonight. You don't think that opera we've just sat through was Jimmy McAphee's idea of a good night's entertainment, do you?'

'Wasn't mine either, come to that,' grunted Edwin Frere.

'The best thing you could do would be disappoint her. Don't get involved with anyone, just talk to your own people and ignore the jerks. It would teach her to stop playing little games.'

'I might, at that,' said Edwin Frere. And he loped off to his own people (of whom there were plenty), leaving me modestly pleased with the hope that I had neutralized one of the threats. I remained there by the bar, holding my drink but not drinking, and tuning in to one after another of the conversations around me.

'If I had my way,' came the thick Ulster tone of Jimmy McAphee, immaculately dressed, and indistinguishable from the upper-crust mob except by the greater force of his personality, 'I'd deport the bleeding lot o' them.'

'*What* a good idea!' said the witless society beauty he was talking to. 'I mean, they do say they want to be Irish, don't they? Why not just shunt them down over the border? You really ought to have a word with the Secretary of State about it!'

'My dear,' said Prince Rupert, to the delectable young thing with whom he was sharing a canapé, he nibbling one end, and she the other, so that their rather long aristocratic noses rubbed in an almost Eskimo ecstasy, 'if you don't now, you vill regret it for the rest off your life.'

'Are you quite sure you're *that* good?' she said, with a giggle and a toss of the head. 'Anyway, I mean, *how*, or rather, gosh! I don't mean how, but I mean *where*?'

'I em staying et Clerridge's,' said the Prince.

'Oh good. Because it would be difficult to do it in Buckingham Palace, wouldn't it, I mean—'

'In Buckingham Pellace I haf never bin able to do it et all,' said Prince Rupert.

'Oh no,' said Lady Dorothy Lowndes-Gore, squeezing her strangulated voice out through her nose like the last bit of toothpaste in the tube, 'that wasn't *this* Lady Glencoe. That was Marjorie, Lady Glencoe. Glencoe has married five times, you know. Marjorie was the fourth, and she was nobody. This is *Edwina*, Lady Glencoe, the *second* wife. Mother of Glenclannish, who's the heir. Edwina's father was Earl of Kilgarvan. Irish title, of course. *Terribly* bad blood. Kilgarvan himself, you know, was practically court-martialled in the First War. And the *mother* . . .'

'Jeremy,' said the Princess, smiling her sweetest and most demure smile, and purring like a cat in sight of the creamer, 'I want you to meet Harry Bayle. Harry is an *awfully* good friend of mine. Harry has a lovely flat down the river, it's absolutely the last word. *Terribly* smart. We go there *often*.'

'Oh yes?' said Jeremy Styles, elegantly at ease, and smiling with utter lack of guile. 'Are you an interior decorator?'

'Oh Jeremy, you are naughty,' giggled the Princess. 'Harry's a Member of Parliament.'

'Oh, *the* Harry Bayle!' said Jeremy, with a totally natural gesture of surprise and admiration that only an actor could have managed. 'This *is* an honour. I did enjoy your speech in the House in the defence spending debate. Splendid stuff. You should have gone on the stage.'

'I saw your new play the other night,' said Harry Bayle, similarly at ease, man to man. 'Very funny indeed, I thought. It should run for years.'

The Princess Helena pouted unprettily.

Jimmy McAphee pushed past me on his way to get a refill, and then, a thought striking him, he swung his thick body around and measured me with his eyes.

'Was it you, then, that rang me?'

I followed suit and measured him with my eyes. Under the elegant clothes the tough, vigorous body had a rather horrible force. Not someone to tangle with on a dark night in the Creggan. But then, I knew that. On the other hand, I didn't feel I had much need to fear the man. He hadn't figured very prominently in the Princess's life over the last few months. And I suspected he was just a rough little go-getter whose eyes couldn't see further than next week, but who marked the course of those seven days very determinedly.

'Yes, it was,' I said, 'Just part of my job. If you think about what I said, it makes sense.'

'Oh aye? Well, as it happens, I'd already decided to lay off the rough stuff and concentrate on my game.'

I was surprised he made any distinction. I murmured: 'Very wise.'

'Mind you, after sitting through that lot tonight I could well fancy a bit of a barny with someone or other. It'd get rid of a lot of steam. By—' he let out his breath in a great expression of disgust. 'To think that people come here for pleasure!'

'If you've paid the price of a dinner for two at the Savoy just to get a seat, you feel bound to enjoy it,' I said. 'Do you see much of the Princess these days?'

'Not so much,' said McAphee. 'I'm not bothered. Needless to say, I wasn't approved of. Not that I'd want to be. That lot! Bleedin' parasites. Anyway, they started to throw her in the way of that witless wonder over there.'

He nodded to the far side of the room, where the Honourable Edwin Frere was spreadeagled against the wall in conversation with Lady Dorothy Lowndes-Gore. His expression was one of petulant boredom, but she was talking with a fierce intensity, a look of almost craving hunger on her face. I supposed she was doing one of her bloodstock low-downs.

'If Helena wants him, she's welcome to him,' said McAphee, apparently without rancour. 'A lot of good he'll do her. Or her him, come to that. She's more tease than come. If I go after a bird I want more than a friendly peck to show for my evening.'

That viewpoint came up in another part of the Crush Bar too.

'Jeremy has the star's dressing-room, of course, and it's absolutely super,' the Princess was saying, showing a rather uninventive technique in her desire to arouse jealousy. 'It's an absolutely marvellous place. We're often there for hours and hours after the performance.'

'Really?' said Henry Bayle, with that friendly, politician's show of interest. 'You must let me come along one night. I've never been backstage in a theatre.'

'Oh, I don't think we're likely to invite you,' giggled the Princess. 'I don't like doing things in threes.'

'Darling, you all too frequently refuse to do things in twos,' drawled Jeremy Styles.

'If you were to come to my castle,' murmured the melancholy Prince Rupert, bending over his supper dish, 'my castle at Krackenburg. High in the Bavarian Elps. Or fairly high in the Bavarian Elps. I vould giff you the time off your life. Tell me you vill come, my dear!'

And he bent his head over her and kissed, succulently, the side of her neck. When he straightened I could scarcely forbear looking at his teeth for traces of blood.

'Jimmy!' said the Princess, in that peremptory tone her voice could take on now and then. 'Come here!'

Jimmy McAphee shambled over, an expression of ferocious amiability on his face.

'Jimmy. I want you to meet two very special friends. This is Harry Bayle, and he's an MP, but he's terribly sweet and—'

'Oh aye. Taken over, have you?' said Jimmy McAphee, extending a large, bone-breaking hand.

'And this is Jeremy Styles. I know you don't go to the theatre, but he's a *wonderful* actor, and altogether—'

'I'm not the complete ignoramus, you know. I see the box now and then. How d'you do.'

'I saw you on the box last Saturday,' said Henry Bayle, with all the slumming-it geniality he could muster from his years of canvassing. 'That was a first-rate goal you scored in the second half.'

'Really perfect timing,' said Jeremy Styles.

Jimmy McAphee smirked, but the Princess looked at all the male conviviality and good-nature around her, and she pouted again, again unprettily. I thought I saw tears in her eyes.

'That,' said the Princess to me, as the people began to thin out, 'was the worst party I've been to in years.'

'That's often the way, isn't it, Ma'am?' I said, easily. 'I remember when I used to go fishing as a boy, I always found the more I was longing to have a fish to play with on the end of my line, the less likely the little blighters were to bite.'

The Princess looked at me narrowly. 'It's *you*,' she said

bitterly. 'You organized it.'

'Oh no, Ma'am. You organized it.'

'Then you undermined it. You went aroun threatening people, or I don't know what. You trie to—what's the word?—defuse things.'

'I certainly did my best, Ma'am. We're both unde strict instructions from the Palace, especially since Jam Brudenell's death. There are to be no headlines. I'm ju doing what I can to carry out those instructions.'

The Princess tried to put on one of her freezin haughty expressions, but it came out as a nasty litt scowl. She stamped her foot.

'Oh, I *hate* you when you're like this. You're s pompous and condescending. You don't have to act like father!'

I looked towards the far corner of the enormous ba where her father was ensconced in a serpentine hudd with his foolish blonde.

'Well,' said the Princess, following my gaze, 'I'd g more fun with him around than I do with you. I'm goir now. No, I don't want you to escort me. I'll go wit Joplin. He's more my age. You stay and talk with Lac Glencoe. Edwina, darling! Perfectly lovely party! I' leaving behind my tame bodyguard. Aren't I generou You can both have a perfectly lovely time talking over th 'thirties together!'

And she sailed down the staircase, leaving m chastened and annoyed, and in the clutches of th dreadful Edwina, who had bustled forward at th Princess's summons, wobbling invitingly close, her colou now more strawberry than ever, with ugly veins in h cheeks and an atmosphere of sweat, powder and stale gi clinging about her.

The end of a perfect day.

'The fact is,' said Edwina (she insisted I call her Edwina

that's she's a spoilt little bitch, and she will simply do anything to get her own way.'

We were draped across a sofa in the corner of the bar, miles from the three or four other couples still left, and ignoring the scowls of the Opera House flunkies ostentatiously clearing up. The night was old, and so was Edwina, but Edwina (unlike the night) was still acting young, and occasionally she would snatch a half-empty glass from the hand of a flunkey and down the contents with a flourish. Then she would nestle her head back down onto my chest with a satisfied gurgle.

'Now in *my* young day,' she went on, 'the Royals still could have fun. *Real* fun. I know, because on occasion I had it with them. You've no idea what they managed to keep out of the papers then. One of them was what we used to call a dope-fiend, and nobody knew till years after he died—nobody who was anybody, I mean. Nowadays the poor things even have their telephones tapped, and they have to spend their nights in railway carriages, I gather.'

'Er—that was denied.'

'Well, I just hope they went first-class,' she swept on, ignoring my interjection. 'The trouble with this young lady is that she gets so little fun she has to manufacture lots of trivial excitements. But excitements came quite easily to us. Oh!' she sighed theatrically down into her bouncing bosom. 'Memories! Memories! I remember once when I was going with Fred Cates—he was a terribly famous racing driver in those days, and I was sharing myself with Willie Portsmouth—that's the father of the present Earl, or was he the grandfather? I forget—anyway, there we were in the pits, having a *tremendous* giggle, and Fred Cates *whirling* round and getting so jealous that eventually he positively stopped and *dragged* me into the car and *round* and round we went, and darling, I thought I was going to be the first woman to be raped at ninety miles an hour. My dear, such *fun* we had!'

'Perhaps the young men of today are not what they were,' I suggested.

'Darling, of course they're not. Even after the war, when I was really unofficial hostess to the Tory party, you know, there were some *splendidly* wild young men. Of course they *do* say that one or two of the present junior ministers . . . but alas I've never *tried* them . . . You don't think Margaret . . . ? No, I suppose not. Well, as I say, in my young days men were men, and they made things happen. Whereas now . . . well, look at tonight. The *silly* young thing insists—as a condition, I ask you!—that I invite all those *quite* unsuitable people! I've nothing against footballers in their *place*, which I needn't specify, but I don't as a rule invite them to my parties. And it's all because she's kept on such a tight *rein*, and so much in the public *eye*, that she has to make absurd little excitements for herself. You know, she promised me such fireworks! Such an explosion! Frankly, I'd have been grateful for a damp squib.'

'You were disappointed?'

'Well, darling, the occasion didn't exactly sparkle, did it? When I write my Memoirs—did I tell you about my Memoirs? I'm just waiting for a reasonable offer. If one is going to bare one's soul and so much more, one does demand more than two thousand five hundred for the spectacle—where was I?—yes, well, as I say when I *do* write them, this evening will not figure as one of the sparkling highlights. And when I *think* of who wanted to come!'

'Oh?'

'I mean, there were *heaps* of people just *dying* for invitations. The Home Secretary, for one. Don't *edge* away—I can't stand a man who *edges*. But the Princess insisted I have these *dreary* young men of hers. And invitations are strictly limited, you know. They're having to look at every *penny* at Covent Garden these days, especially with the new GLC on their backs. You noticed the quality of the whisky, I suppose. Boy! Bring that here, darling boy! Drinkies not quite finished! Yes, as I say, that's what makes me so bitter. When I think who rang me up just *angling* for an invitation. Presentable people, who could be *useful*. I know for a start that Gainsborough was just dying to come. And Aberdare.'

It came to me in a flash.

'I'm less interested in Gainsborough and Aberdare than in Oldham and Leamington,' I said.

'Well naturally,' said Lady Glencoe.

'And in Stourbridge, and Nuneaton, and Cumberland.'

'But of course,' said Edwina. 'They're using her quite shamelessly. I wonder you haven't been on to them long ago.'

CHAPTER 15

Two Pieces in the Puzzle

I had to hand it to the old bag: she'd given me the first real illumination I'd had during the entire case.

Because, of course, there it was: the five names on Bill Tredgold's list were not names of places, but *people* – people with titles. Granted the exalted nature of the circles I had been moving in, I really should have thought of that earlier. And as I came to ponder over this new thought (ignoring the gropings and the pointed invitations from the bundle of old gin bottles snuggling around my midriff), I felt I should have latched on to the connection right from the beginning. I'd been told that

Edwin Frere was a younger son of the Earl of Leamington.

Edwin Frere . . . This brought him very close indeed to the centre of the stage. I began to wish that I had Lady Dorothy's stiff-necked expertise in the ramifications of the noble families. Who exactly were all these people, and what was their connection with each other?

I said it aloud: 'What's the connection?'

'Oh, darling, I can't tell you exactly,' said the thick, slurred voice from below. 'They're related somehow, and terribly in with each other, you know?' She straightened up, which was a mercy. 'Let's see – they must be cousins. That's it. Leamington's mother and Cumberland's mother were sisters. Famous Edwardian society beauties, and you know what *that* means: given the bedroom next to the King's for a weekend party in Norfolk, then they were made for life.'

'What was their name?'

'Oh darling, don't stretch the poor old memory at this time of night. Brackenbury. The Brackenbury sisters. One caught an Earl and the other caught a Marquess. I knew them vaguely in my young days, though by then the beauty was definitely a case of the memory lingering on.'

'But what about Stourbridge and Nuneaton?'

'Darling, don't you know *any*thing? Where have you been all your life? Sons, of course . . . My dear, look at that man! That's whisky!'

As luck would have it, an Opera House attendant was passing with my own glass of whisky, still full.

'Here, darling,' Edwina shrieked to him. 'Me me me. Pretty please! Oh thank you, you gorgeous boy. Who can have been so ungrateful as to leave all this?'

'I rather think it was me.'

'Ah, saving yourself for me. How sweet!'

She clearly had no thoughts of the need to save herself for me, for she downed half the glass in a single, experienced swig. From this point on, the interview deteriorated very rapidly.

'Ooops,' she giggled tipsily. 'Him plenty potent firewater.'

'But what,' I said quickly, getting in while she still had a quarter of her wits about her, 'have they been doing?'

'Darling,' she said, breathing fumes into my face as she gazed up in drunken infatuation. 'Everybody knows . . . they've been using her quite shamelessly . . . We all know that.'

Everybody knows. Everybody who was part of that 'all'. Everybody in that tight little circle. Only the police didn't know, and the press, and the general public. And presumably, it must be said, Buckingham Palace.

'But what,' I repeated, 'were they actually using her *for*?'

She downed the second half of her drink, and her speech became slurred to the point of inaudibility.

'Darling, *I* don't know exactly what it was . . . We all just knew there must be something . . . knowing them . . . the way they had got themselves *in* . . . always *there* . . . around her . . . They'd taken her over . . . one doesn't enquire *what* . . . Darling, don't *inquisit* . . . Let the little bitssh sshtew in her own . . . Put your arms around me, baby . . . Comfort your little 'Wina . . . Sleepybye's time, eh? . . .'

And her glass fell on to the sofa, and she slumped down over my lap, not merely asleep, but snoring.

It's a hell of an embarrassing position to be in, sitting there stone cold sober with a mountain of pulsating aristocratic flesh sprawled over you and emitting noises like bathwater going down some Brobdingnagian plug-hole. We were now, thank God, the last guests in the Crush Bar, but I could hardly look the attendants in the face. They all knew the problem, however, and one of them took pity on me.

'Give her two minutes,' he said, 'and then nothing w
wake her.'

I did as I was told, then gently disentangled mysel
When I was finally on my feet poor Edwina was face dov
against the arm of the sofa, so as gently as I could I la
the survivor of Glencoe on her back, and left her lookir
at the ceiling, rather as if she were inspecting th
chandelier. I ran a finger round my shirt collar ar
thanked the attendant.

'I'd rather sit through the bombing of Dresden than g
through that again,' I said.

'You should complain. You were one of the lucky ones
the attendant said with gloomy relish. 'I could tell yc
some stories . . .'

But I didn't let him. I never went much on horror tale
I escaped down the staircase and out into the nigh
leaving them drawing straws as to who should stic
around until she woke.

But it was no sleep yet for me. I knew I wouldn't shu
my eyes until I had sorted out the connections between a
the names on Bill Tredgold's list. I drove straight t
Victoria and the Yard, and plodded along the hal
deserted corridors to the library—open all night, thoug
without professional attendance. Still, I knew roughl
what I needed. With the help of the catalogue I found m
way to the appropriate part of the Reference Section, an
humped out Burke's Peerage, Debrett, The Lande
Gentry, and a few other related volumes. I'd never bee
so grateful for my training as a weight-lifter as when
lugged the enormous volumes back to my office. Wh
says the aristocracy is dying out? I dropped them with
heavy thud on to my desk and got stuck into the research

Once I found my way around the various methods c
entry, and the abbreviations, things began to seem easie
It had been roughly as the divine Edwina had said. Tw
Edwardian beauties, the Brackenbury sisters, ha

married into the aristocracy, and their husbands, in the fullness of time, had become respectively Marquess of Cumberland and Earl of Leamington. George, the present Marquess (born 1920), and John, the present Earl (born 1915), were their sons. The heir of the Marquess of Cumberland was Lord Stourbridge (born 1944), and the heir of the Earl of Leamington was Lord Nuneaton (born 1938). The Honourable Edwin Montague Frere was the Earl's third and youngest son (born 1954), by a second marriage.

Lord Oldham was a different kettle of fish at first sight: he was that lowliest of blue-blooders, a life peer (the sort of thing that hardly gets you more than a frosty nod from the head waiter at the Savoy). He had been enpurpled in the Resignation Honours List of Sir Alec Douglas Home, after serving his party as Under-Secretary at the Ministry of Agriculture and Fisheries, Deputy Chairman (Midlands) and obedient lobby-fodder all his years as MP for Middleford. He had since been Lord Lieutenant of Cheshire, and had served in all sorts of puffed-up local capacities. But his name was Richard Fergusson Frere, and he was the younger brother of the present Earl. No doubt he had served the family interests in the Commons, while the Earl had done similar selfless service in the Lords.

So all that could be summed up in the manner of the old history books (we had *very* old history books at my school) by the following family tree:

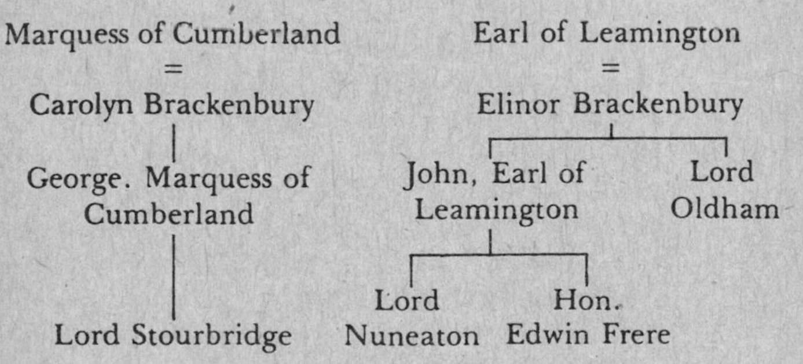

All this was satisfactorily neat. Practically like Mr Bunn the baker and his family. A nice little inter-related network, all tied up together. But tied up in what, for God's sake?

I thought back to the letter Brudenell had been writing at the moment he died:

> Dear John, I must tell you, with great regret, that I can no longer . . .

Was it to the present Earl of Leamington? If so, was it significant in any way at all? What could he no longer do? Why was he typing it as his murderer shot him?

I had got to this point when Joplin strolled in.

'Hello, hello,' I said. 'Back from the Palace? And how did you make out with the Princess? She seemed to be happy to be with someone of her own age at last.'

'I just dropped her at the Palace,' said Joplin airily, as if it was a casual date he'd driven home. I forbore to say that it seemed to have taken him an extraordinarily long time. 'I just looked in here to see if anything had emerged at the party.'

'As a matter of fact, something did,' I said. 'Things march. Come over here.'

And I showed him my little family tree, pointing one by one to the names on Bill Tredgold's list. I think I must have looked smug because Joplin (who is short on reverence and respectful address) said:

'Good heavens. Someone must have put you on to that.'

'It was my own natural detective instincts put me on to it,' I lied.

'I bet it was that old bag of jelly who threw the party. She looked the type who'd tell you anything in return for a quick bang in the back seat.'

'There's no back seat of any car in existence that would accommodate the bulks of her and me engaged in a quick bang, as you horribly call it. You're getting very uppish, Joplin, now you've become a Royal Favourite. That is an honourable position when it is a woman, considerably less honourable when it is a man.'

'The burdens our sex labours under,' grinned Joplin.

'You'd do better to sit down and think what the connection is between this little family network and our Hedda Gabler of Kensington Palace.'

'Who's Hedda Gabler?'

'A Norwegian lady who found Norway so boring she took to manufacturing her own excitements. Come on, get to thinking what it is this little lot is involving Helena in.'

Obedient for once, Joplin sat down and thought.

'They're trying to marry her off to the repulsive Edwin?' he suggested, without much hope.

'Oh, come off it, Garry. They may well be, but that's not a crime. You don't get to marry royalty without a bit of manoeuvring. Life in those spheres is not all Barbara Cartland, even for Barbara Cartland. And remember, we've got two murders on our hands. You've got to come up with something better than the marriage game.'

'I wasn't very hopeful you'd bite at that,' Garry said equably. He went back to thinking, and so did I. Eventually Garry said:

'Why *Operation Seneca*?'

I shrugged. 'Just a joke, I suppose. All those military operations with code names: Operation Crossbow; Operation Cicero. You know. The thriller writers often invent them to get a good title.'

'Yes, I know that. But why Seneca? Who was he?'

'Roman writer of some kind,' I said, vaguely off-hand because in fact I didn't know much more than that. 'There's an encyclopædia over there.'

Joplin took it down from the shelf and browsed through the entry on Seneca.

'Committed suicide on Nero's orders,' he said. 'Very obliging of him. You don't think it could be significant?

Suicide has figured in this case, after all.'

'*Faked* suicide,' I pointed out. 'Happening *after* Tredgold's own death. You're not making much of a case. I expect he just thought it sounded right – reminded him of Operation Cicero.'

'Did he have a classical education?' asked Joplin.

'I shouldn't think so. Latin and Greek are about on a par with theology in the educational world these days.' However, I idly reached over and consulted his file.'Sorry, take that back. His A-levels were French, History and Latin. Went on to read History at Birmingham University.'

'You see,' said Joplin.

'I suppose you're right. With that sort of educational background you probably wouldn't just use the name haphazardly. In fact, Tredgold doesn't seem to have been the type to do anything haphazardly. I'll go along with you: the name must have a meaning, but what the hell it could be I haven't a clue.'

I took the encyclopædia over to my side of the desk and went through the entry myself.

'Philosopher . . . wrote tragedies . . . was tutor to Nero. That must have been an even dicier job than the one we've got now. Committed suicide by opening a vein. A noble, Roman way to go. I don't see what we can make of any of that.'

Joplin shook his head in agreement, but still looked dissatisfied. 'There's got to be something,' he said. 'Is it just the name, perhaps? What does it *mean*?'

'The name? It's just his name. I don't suppose it *means* anything at all.'

'English names do,' Joplin pointed out. 'Like Thatcher means your great-great-great put the roofs on cottages.'

'I'm afraid I don't know a blind thing about Latin names,' I said ungraciously.

'It's just that . . . I don't know . . . there's something in he back of my mind . . . What does the word "senescent" nean?'

'It means something like "connected with old age". You nust have heard it over the last week or two. It has the ame sort of root as "senile" and "senior". Some Latin vord like *senex*, I think . . . Good Lord!'

Garry looked at me: 'You don't think . . . ?'

And I looked at him, gaping. 'I don't know what to hink. I just can't see . . . Hold on a tick. I'm going back o that library.'

It was more than a tick before I got back. Information n Latin names was hard to come by without expert ssistance. When I did get back, I was in a mood of rather .ubious exaltation.

'Who'd be a scholar?' I said. 'That was bloody hard vork. But as far as I can gather, the name Seneca ndicated a sort of branch or subdivision of a larger family God!—I'm beginning to sound like Lady Dorothy). And s meaning derives from *senex*, or old—in a pejorative ense.'

'Talk bloody English.'

'Talk bloody respectfully to your senior, who is not yet enescent. It means something a bit sneery—like "old oy", "old geezer", "gaffer"—you know the sort of thing. But the main thing is, it means something to do with the old.'

'Which, you might say, the Princess is.'

'You might indeed. Oh God, what's the connection . . . 'm just remembering that bod at the Palace. What did e say? "We don't specialize . . . Has she been overdoing it n that direction?" Something like that.'

'What was it Bill Tredgold had been working on just efore he died?'

'Failures of the Welfare State, and that kind of ning . . . neglected old people, hypothermia, appalling Homes . . . There's a connection, if only we can pin it own.'

'Wasn't he interested in local government corruption, and that kind of thing?'

'He was indeed. Oh, there's something there, you know. Something Tredgold was on to, something he was killed for. Garry, let's call it a night.'

'I'm easy on that.'

'I'll leave a message here, asking for all the files on the various noble bigwigs to be on my table tomorrow.'

'You don't think they'll have done time for anything?'

'I do not. Still, we can have hopes for the future. It would improve the tone of Pentonville no end. And I'll have them get the details of all the charities connected with the old that the Princess has been undertaking appearances for.'

'Aid for the Elderly, and all that?'

'That's the ticket.'

'When I went to their AGM they all seemed perfectly sincere and well-meaning do-gooders.'

'There is nothing in the world so easy to fool as a sincere and amiable do-gooder. What I want is a list of all the upper echelons and office-holders. Do you know, Garry, my boy, I see light at the end of the tunnel.'

CHAPTER 16

Henry Shorthouse Tucker

And in the morning, there it all was waiting for me, in a neat little folder sent up from records. I opened it with a feeling of expectation hardly at all damped by having had very little sleep. Needless to say, on the five noble lords the sheets were entirely blank. Their careers were, to the public eye, blameless. Edwin Frere had been questioned a couple of times—about gambling debts, and a default on a loan. Nothing had come of either episode. I didn't doubt that on both occasions he had been handled with the double-thickness kid gloves the police do put on when dealing with people with titles, position, or clout of any kind. I could just imagine all the 'Sorry you've been troubled's' that were flying round.

But the prospectuses and PR material for Aid for the Elderly were decidedly more interesting. It was a nationwide enterprise, but it was divided into regions. On the national committee, along with MPs, newspaper editors, senior television executives and committed radical novelists, I found the Earl of Leamington and Lord Stourbridge listed as Vice Presidents. As President of the South Midlands regional group I noticed the Marquess of Cumberland, and as Honorary Secretary of the North Midlands region I found Lord Nuneaton. Lord Oldham was chairman of the fund raising committee (Midland region). Clearly they were a family united, nay single-minded, in their determination to serve the old. All the regional groups bulged with names which had a vaguely familiar ring—business people, mostly, I suspected, with a sprinkling of senior sportsmen, local politicians and suchlike.

But one name interested me particularly, and it wasn't one of the Frere clan at all. If I was right about what had been going on, the king-pin position had to be that of Treasurer. I looked at the prospectus (Midland region) and saw the following:

'Treasurer (Midlands): Henry Shorthouse Tucker (M.I.Ch.A)' Something seemed to ring a very tiny bell.

'Garry,' I said, when he came in, 'does the name Tucker mean anything to you?'

He thought.

'Not in isolation. Shall I get the computer on to it?'

We have a computer at the Yard, with all manner of names and aliases used by all manner of villains over the last thirty or forty years. Mostly it isn't working; when it is, it feeds you back so much info that you spend weeks sorting through it for the nugget you actually want.

'No,' I said. 'I leave the mechanized future to the younger boys. I'll remember in a second . . . Do you remember that entry in Bill Tredgold's notebook: "Treasurer". We thought it might refer to one of the local government cases he was also dealing with at the time, but I think we were wrong. Garry, it's an off-chance, but could you get me the Shropshire telephone directory?'

Off-chance it may have been, but there it was:

'Tucker, Henry S., 9, Clunbury Lane, Knightley.' And it was then that I remembered.

'Garry—I've got it. It was before your time—mostly before mine too, but there was a marvellous little crook, confidence trickster, call him what you like, who had as many aliases as the Queen has titles, but who as often as not used the name Tucker.'

'Would that be Jimmy Hopgood?' asked Garry.

'You're right. How on earth did you know about him?'

'I heard about him from my Dad. He was in the force, you know. He nabbed him absconding with a load of bets from Aintree.'

'That'd be Jimmy.'

So we sat down and chewed the cud over everything we could remember about Jimmy Hopgood.

He was first and foremost a master of disguise. Not the crude stuff, with dark glasses and false moustaches. When Jimmy Hopgood took on a new name and a new game, he took on a new personality. I remembered him as Simeon B. Tucker, a slow, anxious, humourless creature, pathetically willing, working for a multi-national with offices on the Embankment. Dim Sim, the other bright sparks in the office called him. Dim Sim had diddled the Nordica Oil Company of something like thirty thousand pounds before that day when he failed to turn up at work and uncharacteristically didn't send in a doctor's certificate either. They never got him. Before that he'd been Harold G. Tucker, tetchy, meticulous, slightly military, a stickler for doing things according to the regulations. He had been employed by the London Northern Bank, and had even risen in a short time to being temporary manager in a small branch in Balham. They got him that time, and got back most of the loot too. Hopgood did four years, and was a model prisoner. He rose to be trusty librarian, and when he left he took with him a disregarded first edition of *Scenes of Clerical Life*, donated and signed by the author. That was his last jail sentence, and since then nothing much seemed to have been heard of him. Earlier on there had been Roger Dashwood Tucker, the Second World War flying ace, down on his luck, Gerald Fitzjames Tucker, the man-about-town with a flair for the Stock Exchange, and Honest Harry Tucker, The Bookie You Can Trust. The changes to his appearance were minimal, which was a disadvantage at identification parades, but an advantage in almost every other way: I have never known false moustaches inspire real confidence. He was a frustrated actor, of course, an actor of the Alec Guinness type; one who submerges himself totally in the character he is playing. I'm quite sure that when he was Simeon B. Tucker he made himself a bedtime cup of cocoa every night, and when he was Honest Harry Tucker he went to bed slightly pissed and didn't aim too well at the loo. There are criminals (even murderers) in the contemplation of whom even the most law-abiding can only stand back and admire; here is an artist. Jimmy Hopgood was one of these.

'And Jimmy Hopgood, I wouldn't mind betting, is now living in semi-retirement in Clunbury Lane, Knightley,' I said.

'Turning a dishonest penny,' agreed Garry. 'If it's him

how old would he be?'

'Sixty-five or so, at a guess. You wouldn't expect Aid for the Elderly to employ a young man.'

'I guess he regards Aid for the Elderly as a charity just made to keep him in a comfortable retirement.'

'Hmmm. Well, I'm afraid that's going to come to an end. But it's not him I'm really interested in, Garry. It's obvious that Hopgood is just a tool. What's more, as I remember him, he was as unlikely a murderer as they come. Still, I'm looking forward to meeting him. I wonder what percentage they give him. Pretty bloody low, if I know my noble families. Well, well, I think today is the day I take off for the Midlands again, Garry.'

Which is what I did. I took the Inter-City to Birmingham, picked up a car from the central police pool, and drove over to Knightley, arriving in good time for afternoon tea. It struck me again as a pleasant village to retire to. The weather was still rather nippy, but some of the good people of Knightley (few of whom were young) were out in their gardens getting on with the little jobs that precede the coming of spring. Henry Shorthouse Tucker was not one of them. If he had been, I suspect he'd have been round the back and out the back gate before I'd got my key out of the ignition. But his garden was neat, the paths well cared for, the roses (which must have been a picture last year) well pruned back. He was obviously in one of his meticulous phases.

I went up the weedless crazy-paved path, and rang the doorbell.

The man who opened the door of the stone-dashed, symmetrical little bungalow was dressed in a neat grey cardigan and well-creased grey flannels, and he peered short-sightedly through rimless spectacles. He was the spit-and-image of the professional gentleman, the professional financial gentleman, in retirement.

'Can I help you?'

'Good afternoon,' I said cheerily. 'It's Jimmy Hopgood, isn't it?'

'I'm afraid you've come to the wrong house,' he said, beginning to shut the door. 'I think there are Hopgoods at number twenty-nine.'

'While you do a bunk out the back gate, eh, Jimmy? Come off it, old chap. I was on duty at the Old Bailey when you were sent down in 'seventy-four. You were Harold S. Tucker then, remember, and you'd just over-reached yourself with the London Northern.'

'I assure you—'

'—you can't think what I'm talking about. Well, you can play it like that if you want to, Jimmy. I can take fingerprints, and we can match them up, and we can go through all the old dance routines. It's just that that kind of game takes time, and I don't think we have it. I'm here to save you from a heap of trouble, Jimmy, so I do think you might invite me in.'

'Trouble?'

'A murder charge, Jimmy.'

It gave him to pause, and he looked straight at me.

'I think you'd better come in.'

I had to stoop to get into the door of that little pre-war bungalow. We stood for a moment in the dark little hall, and as my eyes got accustomed to the gloom, I saw a suitcase standing by the door into the kitchen.

'All ready for a getaway, I see, Jimmy?'

'I had contemplated a short vacation,' he said with dignity. His voice, for this role, was high, precise, and replete with a genuine middle-class respectability.

'I can't make any promises about duration,' I said. He sighed.

'Come into the sitting-room.'

We sat down in comfortable, auction-sale armchairs, in a neat, rather characterless room, the furniture solid, at the window, lace curtains, those guardians of the middle class's secret life, or lack of it.

'I suppose it's no use offering you a cup of tea?'

'Not if there's a back door. Come on, Jimmy. Let's get this over as soon as possible. It's obvious you've been expecting a call.'

Jimmy sighed again. 'I supposed it was too much to hope that your last visit here would indeed be your last.'

'Ah, you heard about that?'

He looked cagey. 'News gets around in a village. I drank elsewhere than the Wrekin on the evening in question, but I should have been wise and got out then, for good. There were considerations, however . . .'

'I bet there were. You saw yourself being set up for the fall guy, and saw that that was even more likely if you made a dash for it. You were very wise. Look, Jimmy, we both know what I'm talking about. Let's get things straight: I'm here to do you a good turn.'

'I have a friend,' said Jimmy, still in his high, articulate voice, 'who maintains that when a policeman says that to you, you should prepare yourself for a stiff sentence.'

'You have cynical friends. Let's face it, Jimmy, you're in trouble. If there was ever anyone set up for a murder charge, it's you: here you are, under a false identity, the Treasurer of a large and rich charity, from whom you are peculating funds. Along comes an investigative journalist, specializing in social abuses of one kind or another. He's done to death in your local pub, in a manner that would have been particularly easy for you to manage. You see—we're half way to making a case already.'

'I admit none of the early part of what you have said,' said Jimmy Hopgood, with lawyer-like pedantry. 'The latter part you clearly don't believe yourself.'

'No, I don't. I don't think you've got the nerve for murder, or the sheer evil-mindedness. But you're caught in an age-old trap. Present the court with an old lag with a record—albeit not half so long a record as he deserves – and give them a choice between him and a noble Lord with an impeccable career of public service, and clean hands all his life – not to say four or five noble Lords – and who do you think they're going to choose to send down? In a way, you can hardly blame them. But I don't want you landed in the stir while those titled con-men get away with it.'

He looked at me quizzically: 'Hard words, Inspector, about men with impeccable reputations.'

'I don't have Snobby Driscoll's respect for the upper crust,' I said. 'What was the Snobby Driscoll connection, by the by?'

'An act of charity,' Hopgood enunciated after a pause, most ill-repaid, it now seems. In fact, I gave him a bed for the weekend, as one old friend to another. He was eighteen months from his earliest parole date, but when cancer was diagnosed they gave him short periods of compassionate leave. His family were mostly dead, or in the stir, and he was always particularly fond of Shropshire.'

'You're all heart, Jimmy,' I said. 'And it really wasn't Snobby gave you away. Now let's get down to the nitty. You've been set up by a ring of particularly clever crooks, and any other policeman would have you in this moment for questioning on a murder charge. With a bit of luck that lot could even manage to wriggle their way out of a peculation charge. I imagine they've been super-circumspect.'

'They have, of course,' agreed Jimmy Hopgood, a slow, sly smile wafting over his face. 'Fortunately, the thought had occurred to me, and I have been still more circumspect. From the beginning I have taken elementary precautions.'

'Good. I'm glad of that. What sort of precautions?'

'Tape-recordings, in point of fact. We communicated only by phone, and I was told to use a public box. I rang them regularly once a week, and otherwise only if an emergency turned up. Such as Bill Tredgold writing to ask for an interview. Unfortunately for them, I usually took along a portable recording machine. Tapes are dicey evidence, of course, but there was also one single letter, with "Burn this" at the bottom. It has no crest, but it is written in the noble gentleman's hand. I treasure it.'

'So you should. Are these things safe?'

'Lodged at my bank. I am a great believer in using the correct procedures. I've got good and trusted friends, but a good friend is never quite as reliable as a good bank.'

'Well, it's nice that with your experience you still believe that. Now, come on, Jimmy, let's have the story from the beginning. There's no point in holding back. We know who you are. We know you're claiming to be a Chartered Accountant, which you're not—'

'I'm a sight better than most of them—'

'—I don't doubt that. And we know you're acting in an official capacity for Aid for the Elderly (and possibly other charities) under a false name. That's quite enough to pull you in for, with more to follow when we go through the books. Wouldn't it be sensible to come clean? As I say, it's not you I'm after, and I'll go all out to get you off as lightly as possible.'

Jimmy, whose Henry S. Tucker personality was thawing off him, but very gradually, screwed up his face in thought.

'I've no cause to do that lot down. They've treated me right, by and large. But if it's murder—'

'It's murder, Jimmy. Two murders.'

'Cripes! I never thought they'd have it in them. You wouldn't think it to look at them, would you?'

'I've not seen them.'

'You've seen one of them. You met Lord Nuneaton, when you went with the Princess to that Old Folks' Home in Birmingham. You stood there talking about horses and dogs.'

'Good God! Was that Nuneaton? I never suspected. You mean you were there too, Jimmy? What were you doing?'

'Merging into the background. I wasn't one of the nobs. Just there in my official capacity.'

'Right then, Jimmy, are you going to come across with it, or shall we get in my car and drive back to the Yard?'

'I'll tell you it, as it happened, though God help me if I rely on your word as a cop. Well, this is it: it's a good luck story really. With an unhappy ending. It started when I was in Churston—you know, the open clink just outside Coventry. Very nice class of place, mostly business frauds and your once-off domestic kind of murder. Well, I'm not getting any younger, you know, and it occurs to me I ought to be looking round for a nice little niche to retire to. They take all the good class papers there for the business frauds, and I see all these ads for Aid for the Elderly, telling the good middle-class readers what a good job they do, and how many pathetic old pieces of won't-lift-a-hand-to-help-themselves they assist to live in happy independence. And just for a lark I writes them a note—pardon me, *write*; how mixing with the police does lower one's standards—I write them a note, on prison paper. All above board—dignified, you know, plain-speaking and honest. Fairly honest. How I'd strayed from the path, but how I was getting old, and was terrified by the thought that I might have to live my last years in gaol, and how I was looking for a humble and honourable retirement. Could they help me?'

'I see. So in a way, you practically applied for the job.'

'Unbeknowing. Right. Well, I expected the coldest of cold shoulders, what with all the deserving hard-up there are around these days. You could have knocked me down with a social security cheque when I get a letter back three or four weeks later saying that if I would contact them at a certain number when I left gaol, they might be able to help me.'

'The number you were to ring not being one of the Society's official phones, I take it.'

'By no means. But I wasn't smelling rats then, and I didn't think twice. I phoned them the day after I was released. I was put on to a very smooth-spoken gent, and an appointment was made. I was told I would meet a young gentleman who might be able to help me.'

'Where were you to meet?'

'A big Birmingham pub called the Dog and Whistle. Acres of space, 'specially at eleven in the morning. I thought it an odd place for a charity to appoint, but I went along, and there I met someone I expect you know. Lad called Edwin Frere.'

'I thought Edwin would be in it too, somewhere.'

'In there kicking. Friend of your little lady, isn't he? That's what they say in the *Grub*. Well, he's a sulky individual, but he was on his best behaviour, and he took me over into a corner miles from the bar, and he was fairly mean with the half pints, but he took me through a long inquisition on my past. What I'd done time for, what I'd got away with, and he got me to talk a lot about my methods and so on. I didn't know what was up, but I told him it all straight. I threw him the complete honesty line. A very useful line in certain circumstances, as I'm sure you've found out yourself.'

'Me?'

'I understand you're a married man. I'm sure you've used that line from time to time. Anyway, he said he'd have to go away and report, and could we meet again next evening. Which we did, and he took me to a minor mansion of some kind, and I had this long talk with your Lord Nuneaton.'

'Who put a proposition to you?'

'Not in so many words. By no means. Nothing was ever said, not directly, you understand . . . we went about it in a gentlemanly fashion . . . roundabout, you might say. It took hours, I tell you. But it came to the same in the end. In return for certain services to them, I would have a respectable position with the Society, get a certain percentage (five) of certain sums (unspecified) which I would convey . . . and so on. And I would get my rent paid. I stood out to have a little place bought for me, and I'm glad I did. They went along with that, because it was more difficult to trace it back to them.'

'I see. And what was involved was a straightforward fiddling of the books?'

'More or less. Initially. You make it sound worse than it was. You've got to remember that something of that sort has been going on for years in their kind of circle. Lady Muck gives her name as Patron of the Distressed Gentlewoman's Needlework Trust. Addresses the AGM with a few well-chosen words of condescension, sticks down the odd envelope once a month. In return, she has the flat above the offices as a nice little free pied-à-terre whenever she happens to be in London. This mob did the same: they lent their names, and very good names for the purpose they are too. They made sure of getting something really good in return.'

'But surely, there wouldn't be enough to make it worth their while?'

'Don't be so sure. It's a very rich charity. The old are a big thing at the moment. Everyone in the country feels that bit guilty, because they don't take care of their oldies like they used. It's guilt money, that's what it is. Then again, I think that even then they had something bigger in mind.'

'Meaning—?'

'Meaning the Princess.'

'I see. It's the Princess I'm really interested in.'

'I thought so. Snobby Driscoll put you on, did he? I could see he was pretty upset when I let it slip while we were jawing. Now as to the details of how she's been involved, I'm a bit at sea. Because of course they never confided in me. Just gave me my instructions by phone, and the odd cool nod if I came to official receptions or AGMs. But the time I came out of Churston was about the time the Princess was beginning to get into the news: snipping the odd tape, visiting the odd oil-rig, you know what I mean. Now, I don't know what the connection was, but they got in there somehow.'

'They certainly did.'

'So that before long, the Princess opened a new Old People's Home somewhere near Coventry. The press fawned, people flocked to see her, and it became the first of lots of such visits. And that's when the money started rolling in. Much of it quite genuine: a royal visit generates publicity, especially, at the moment, one by her. Publicity generates donations, quite spontaneously. A discreet amount—in fact, quite considerable amounts—of that inflow could be siphoned off. But then there was the other . . .'

'Yes?'

'Well, wherever Royalty goes, there's people anxious to meet them, shake the royal hand, have a few words to take back and tell their grandchildren or their neighbours. Particularly their neighbours. And they're even more anxious to meet them on an informal basis—over cocktails, after the official side of the visit is over. And it wasn't long before the local businessmen realized that the way to the Princess was through the Leamington/Cumberland crowd. And when they approached them—'

'—it became a straight cash transaction, I suppose?'

'Not directly. Nothing so vulgar as bargaining. Of course there was no question of someone like

Leamington, or someone like Nuneaton, being bribed. All they wanted was donations to Aid for the Elderly. Better make it anonymous, eh? In case questions were asked. You send it direct to the Treasurer, and I'll do what I can, old boy. Shall we say a couple of thousand? And I think I can promise you . . . Very smoothly done, as you'd expect with that crowd. I get the money, deduct my percentage, and hand the rest straight back. Nothing to trace, no questions asked. In my annual accounts I include a discreetly large sum under "anonymous donations". Everybody's happy.'

'A very nice little game.'

'I thought so. I couldn't have dreamed up a better myself. But then, I had their cheek but I don't have their connections. There were other little sidelines too. For a really whacking sum, ten or fifteen thou, they would try and get the Princess to visit some particular factory, or store, or warehouse, or whatever. This was much more difficult to bring off, and they didn't try it very often. After all, the guest list at receptions after an old folks visit could be fiddled at this end, but the engagements were decided on in London, by the Princess's people.'

'True. Still, they must have had a connection there. Presumably Brudenell, the Princess's private secretary. Funny. He was a fussy, infuriating little body, but I wouldn't have thought him crooked. And the poor bloke's dead . . . Did you know anything about that end of things?'

'Not a thing. I was given the absolute minimum of info, as I said. I was useful to them because I did what I was told and held my tongue. I imagine they must have had the Secretary in their pockets. Or perhaps the young lady herself: she looks an expensive little thing. Perhaps she got her cut, as a nice little addition to the Civil List.'

'That thought is downright disloyal, Jimmy: Snobby Driscoll would have had you by the throat if you'd suggested that to him. I must say, I'd hardly have thought it worth her while, quite apart from anything else. In fact, I'm surprised it has been worthwhile for this mob.'

'It's a very, very rich charity, I tell you, Mr Trethowan. And by now they're doing very nicely at it indeed, and I'm the one who'd know. When the present Earl of Leamington's father died, they had to sell bits of the ancestral loot. The Cumberland lot are hard up anyway: the family seat became a loony-bin not long after the war. They've got wise to all sorts of dodges, and of course the elder sons have taken over all the doings already, to avoid death duties. I sometimes wonder whether there's a nobleman in the country ever dies worth more than a couple of quid these days. But there are younger sons very much unprovided for. I wouldn't mind betting a lot of the dibs has gone in little Edwin's direction.'

'That would be pouring money down the drain.'

'Not if they tied it up for him.'

'Why do you think it went to him?'

'The general gossip around the charitable cocktail circuit. A late baby, doted on by the present Earl and by his second wife. Some kind of step-sister worshipping the ground he walked on, and even Lord Nuneaton turning a blind eye to all sorts of shabby tricks. It's difficult to see his fatal attraction, isn't it?'

'Very. But it's not difficult to see that kind of upbringing leading to that kind of young man. Was he in on the Aid for the Elderly organization at any level?'

'Not on your life. They had to have solid, respectable names. He's about as credit-worthy as a Salvation Army dosser.'

'Pity. That'll make it that much more difficult to pin anything on him. You had no dealings with him after that first interview?'

'Not a thing.'

'We can't make much of a charge out of that . . . Well,

well, I think I can leave that to the Birmingham Police. I'll have to deliver you over to them too, Jimmy.'

'I knew it. The word of a policeman—'

'Look, Jimmy, I've got no option. This is serious stuff. I'll put in all the good words for you there are in the book, and I'll come to your trial, if it comes to that.'

'If I gave you my word of honour I'd stay put here—?'

'Words of honour went out in the nineteenth century, Jimmy, and I doubt if yours would have buttered many parsnips even then. Besides, would you really want to stay here?'

'What's wrong with it? Nice little nest it is, and it's mine.'

'No doubt. But news travels, as you've said. Think what happened to Bill Tredgold when he started showing interest. What do you think they'll try and do when they hear that I've been round talking to you?'

'I'll get my bag. It's all packed,' said Jimmy Hopgood.

CHAPTER 17

The Figure in the Frieze

As I said to Garry Joplin the next morning, everything began to make sense, except the main riddle.

'The peculation side of it is not really our baby at all, and I've left that in the hands of the Midlands police. With some misgivings, I may say. Left to themselves, they'd probably have slapped a charge on Jimmy Hopgood and regarded the rest of it as pure moonshine.'

'They gave you the "These are respected local citizens" line and all that, I suppose?'

'Not to mention the "These families have been in this area for centuries" line. Why that should seem even to the dimmest intelligence to be a sure-fire certificate for probity I cannot imagine. I had to force them to get hold of the tapes before they'd even begin to take it seriously. Then I had to bring in the threat to the Princess, and emphasize that these toffs were part of it. If they were going to pull rank, I could pull a higher one. They'll be interviewing some of the Frere family now. When the forelock-touching had to stop! I would like to be there. But meanwhile we're left with our part of the problem.'

'But we must be nearly there,' said Garry Joplin, spreading himself out in the only easy chair in my office. 'Surely we can take it that Tredgold was on to them, and that was why he was killed; that Brudenell was in with them but wanting out, and that was why he was killed. And the obvious deduction is, that one of the gang of five killed them, or very possibly Edwin Frere.'

'I suppose so. But even accepting that, it leaves the big question of which? And I must say, I just can't make myself happy with that explanation.'

'Why?'

'For no very pin-downable reason. Just a feeling of dissatisfaction. Did Brudenell strike you as a crook? Did he strike you as someone willing to take big risks? Did he strike you as someone likely to put his whole standing and reputation at risk?'

'No . . .' admitted Garry, slowly and unwillingly. 'Definitely not, I suppose . . . He seemed quite honourable, in his rather ridiculous way . . . And something of a coward too. But then, if pressure was put on him . . . What exactly was the connection?'

I shoved a hefty volume in his direction.

'Oh, it's all there, in the Landed Gentry. I should have looked him up at once. He was just the sort who would make sure he was in, in full detail. There was a distant connection with the Leamingtons—his father was a second cousin twice removed, or something, of the then

Earl, father of the present one. I've phoned St Paul's School: it was that Earl who paid for Brudenell's schooling.'

'Well, that's it, isn't it?' said Garry, who like all young people is easily satisfied. 'The present lot called for the payment of an old debt. Brudenell, torn between gratitude and conscience—'

'Spare me the Victorian scenarios. All right. I agree it could be something like that. But I would much prefer to believe that Brudenell was got into the job by the Old Boy network—he was already part of the royal stable, remember—but that once he was in he was *used* rather than pressured—used, while he himself remained quite unaware of what was going on. He was a foolish man, and foolish enough for that. All that was involved was the patronage of a perfectly respectable charity, and the odd minor favour to a noble relative. It's when he became aware of what was behind it all that he began to make trouble.'

'How did he become aware?'

'One of his pals in the real upper crust, more cynical than he was, tipped him off, perhaps? Or the fact that I was around, snooping, asking about the Princess's engagements, made him more aware? Oh, and McPhail found a letter in his files from one of the other charities for the old, complaining of favouritism.'

'Right. That's convincing enough. Then he starts looking at his scrapbook and sees just how out of proportion things have been getting, and realizes it could come right back to him. Then he starts to make trouble, and one of them comes along to his flat and shoots him.'

'I think that must be basically right. One of the lesser lights—I mean one of the younger ones—comes to Whitehaven Mansions, perhaps by appointment, and Brudenell charges him with what he thinks has happened. That fits in well with what Malcolm Woodley told us. When this is admitted, Brudenell says he will write immediately to Lord Leamington—I suppose he has had enough to do with him recently to allow even Brudenell to begin his letter "Dear John", though he must in fact have been something of a revered elder figure for him earlier on. He starts to write that there will be no question of the Princess being used in this way in the future. While he is typing, the other man in the room shoots him.'

'Yes. That fits all right, doesn't it?'

'No, it *doesn't*. Not as it stands. The murderer—try to visualize it—reaches over, takes Brudenell's gun from the drawer, stands close beside him and shoots him, while Brudenell has apparently gone on typing. We know he was bent over the machine from the angle of the bullet. Can you imagine it?'

Obviously Garry couldn't, but he made the attempt.

'Perhaps he used some trick. Covered up with conversation.'

'Like "What a pretty little gun you have here. Do you mind if I play with it?" No, Garry. If the murderer was apparently any innocent visitor that might wash, but it won't work for someone Brudenell has just had an argument with over an important matter of principle.'

'What's your solution?'

'I haven't got one . . . Another gun? One similar or identical to Brudenell's?'

'Where the hell would you get one like that in this country?'

'I know, I know. Nothing I come up with works out any better than the solution we've got already.'

In my dissatisfaction at myself I was fiddling with the papers I had found on my desk that morning. I had been so eager to toss the thing about with Garry that I hadn't looked at them, but now, frustrated by the feeling that something was staring me in the face that I was failing to recognize, I took up one of the reports idly and began to read it.

'Good God!' I said.

'What?'

'The Shrewsbury police have actually come up with something. The matter of the two glasses and the bottle of wine. They finally went to the top. I suppose I should have told them to do that at the beginning, remembering the class we're dealing with. The Carlton—the most exclusive hotel in Shrewsbury. A waiter in the dining-room there remembers a customer, alone, ordering wine and dinner for two. When he came with the meal, the two glasses, the bottle and the customer had disappeared. Three ten pound notes had been left on the table. Doesn't remember the date, of course, but it would be some time before Christmas.'

'Good Lord. I suppose he remembers nothing at all about the customer?'

'Not in detail. I'd distrust him if he did. But he remembers one whoppingly important fact.'

'What?'

'The customer was a lady.'

It took a moment or two to rearrange my ideas. That sort of thing always stuns you for a moment. Then, when the mist cleared, I felt that at long last I was no longer clutching at straws, that a coherent pattern was forming in my head.

'Garry, Garry, it could just work out. I could be on the right lines at last. Those guns—'

'What guns?'

'The identical guns—come *on*, lad, we were talking about them a minute ago. Those two identical guns, bought *at the same time* in America, by two people, strange to the country, nervous at being out on the streets, nervous in their hotel rooms—'

'Good God—'

'Garry. Hand me the Burke's.' And I riffled throug
the pages until I found it. 'There. The ninth Ear
Reresby, who married Pamela Dorothy Frere, the sister o
the present Earl of Leamington. Both killed in an ai
crash in Southern Spain in 1955.'

'Well?'

'The family name is Lowndes-Gore.'

'Christ! I thought you were talking about the Princess.

'And Lady Dorothy is their only daughter.'

'I don't believe it. Not Lady Plum-in-the-throat.'

'It must be. It fits. Lady Glencoe talked about then
being all around her. This was what she was talkin
about. I bet Lady Dorothy was brought up by her uncle
Jimmy Hopgood talked about some kind of step-sister t
Edwin. I bet that's her. Go back to what we were jus
talking about. Brudenell finds out that he's been used
Asks her to visit him to talk it over. She puts it in the bes
light possible, but he's still full of self-important rage. H
proclaims his intention of writing to the Earl, and whil
he types the first words, she pulled out her *own* gun fron
her handbag, shoots him, puts his prints on it, and ther
takes his gun from his desk. She'd visited him before
Perhaps they'd talked about where they both kept thei
souvenirs of the States.'

'You've no sort of case.'

'None at all. But I've got more than enough excuse fo
talking to her. What's the Princess doing today?'

'Visit to a repertory theatre in East Grinstead. The nev
lady-in-waiting in attendance.'

'The *what*?'

'The new lady-in-waiting. They swap regularly, yo
know, two of them doing three months or so at a time
Ordinary mortals can only stand so much of th
boredom. I heard from Kensington Pal that the new on
took over today.'

'Right. Then I'm going over there, case or no case.'

And leaving Garry behind, because I thought the lady would talk more freely to me alone, I drove through the silvery February sunshine till I turned into Palace Avenue, drove past the check-point and up to the back entrance of the Palace. As luck would have it, a flunkey was loading a leather suitcase into the back of a limousine, and as I got out of my police car Lady Dorothy emerged from the Palace and walked purposefully towards the Rolls. I cleared my throat.

'Oh, Lady Dorothy—'

'Ye-e-es?' She looked down her long Roman nose as she forced the word through, and I could imagine icicles forming from it, making her into a weird surrealist portrait. But then I looked into her eyes, and the tasteful make-up could not disguise the pinkness of them.

'I wonder if I might have a word with you?'

'I'm afraid no-ot,' she drawled, in her characteristic dying fall. 'I have a train to catch in three-quarters of an hour.'

The flunkey by the car was three or four yards away, and I murmured:

'Lady Dorothy, I don't know if you know that your cousin is at present being questioned by the Birmingham Police.'

She cast me a frozen look.

'Yes. My uncle rang. Some dreadful little man has been helping himself to charitable funds. Nuneaton is helping them look into it. Such a bore for him, but he is Honorary Secretary. I'm sure it will be cleared up in no time.'

'Hardly,' I said. 'The dreadful little man taped all his conversations with your cousin, and one or two with your uncle. Not to mention the Cumberlands. I think you had better let me drive you to the station.'

She hesitated for a moment. It was the first crack I had ever seen in her massive composure. Then she walked over to the flunkey.

'Will you put my luggage in Superintendent Trethowan's car? He'll drive me to King's Cross.'

Without an ill-bred flicker the flunkey began to transfer her luggage, and we stood there in the sunshine talking as if this were the most casual of encounters. I said: 'Are you going far?'

'To Scotland. We have a little place there.'

'Very nice,' I said.

Then she got in and we drove off.

'We haven't much time, Lady Dorothy, and I don't intend to go about things in a polite way, because that takes hours. I want to tell you what I think has been happening. I believe that you have been using your position, through James Brudenell, to ensure that the Princess can be of financial benefit to your family. I take it for granted this has been without her knowledge. I think Brudenell, in spite of the fact that your family was probably instrumental in getting him the job, was also quite unaware of the use you were putting him to. I think you and your uncle and your cousins used him in a very subtle, indirect way, and he was quite happy to be of service. Your family were also, remotely, his, and the present Earl's father was a sort of benefactor. I don't know how this state of things came to an end. I do know that the way your family were crowding in on the Princess became general gossip among people of your class.'

So far she had sat in the front seat gazing stonily ahead of her, but now she blinked at my impertinence.

'However, he came to realize what had been happening—whether by this gossip, or my investigation, or however. When he did begin to suspect, he started thinking about things, he consulted his scrapbook and saw how lop-sided the Princess's engagements had become. He made discreet enquiries. Eventually he asked you to call at his flat, and he told you it had to stop. To prove his determination, he began to write a letter to your uncle. You shot him with a gun you had bought in America, bought when you were in the Princess's entourage together with him. Then you substituted it for his own identical or near-identical gun. It may not have been difficult for you. You had killed before. You had learnt from the Princess that Bill Tredgold had been asking inconvenient questions. You heard from your family that he had requested an interview with the so-called Henry Tucker. You made sure that he never got to that interview.'

She still gazed stonily ahead at the early tourists in Shaftesbury Avenue, as if the story were a fiction, told to while away the journey.

'I have no evidence of this,' I said. 'I shall do my damnedest in the weeks ahead to get evidence. I only hope I can do that without harming the reputation of the Princess. You know how some people are willing to seize on anything . . .'

Her eyes went sideways to my face, and then fixed themselves again on the road ahead. Then suddenly she started to speak, in that low, nasal, squeezed-out voice, quite drained of all obvious emotion.

'My father and mother were killed when I was six. I was a very lonely child, even before that. They were social people, very gay. When they were killed, I went to live with my Uncle John. My nanny was pensioned off, so I had nobody I knew left. My Uncle John had married again, a young wife. They were often in London, or on the Continent. The other children were nearly grown up. The servants looked after me. I was not an attractive child. Then Uncle John and Aunt Elizabeth had a child. A son. He was a lovely baby. I nursed him—more than his own nanny. I taught him, brought him up, loved him. I had never had anyone to love before, but now I could love him more than anything in the world. Edwin grew up such a handsome boy. When he went away to school, I just lived from day to day, waiting for the holidays. When he asked for something, I fetched it for him. When he called me, I ran to him. When he kissed me goodbye and went back to school I cried for days. People are always telling me now that Edwin is no good. I don't believe them. And even if I did, it would make no difference. For me he is everything good—the supreme good.'

She paused, as we were arriving at King's Cross. I looked at my watch, and then drove on, around the station.

'When my cousin Nuneaton told me they had a plan, he said it was to make some kind of independence for Edwin. I never asked for details. I just did what they told me. I'm sure—*quite* sure—Edwin himself knew nothing about it. I don't myself believe any great harm has been done. I expect most people they got money out of knew perfectly well what was going on . . . I don't know how I should bear it, if members of my family went to prison . . .'

'And the other matter? The murders?'

Her mouth set itself in an obstinate line. 'I won't say anything about those . . . As you say, the Princess must not be harmed.'

'I shall try to see that she isn't. If it can be avoided.'

'Mr Trethowan.' Suddenly there was a real urgency in her voice for the first time. 'May I ask you not to make your investigations too quickly? Too energetically? . . . The cottage to which I am going is very old . . . we cook by gas . . . It's old and defective.'

'As at Knightley?'

'Yes. As at Knightley. But I shall need *time* . . . to summon up . . . courage. Will you promise me that?'

I drove on, silent.

'Mr Trethowan, we are coming to the station again. The train leaves in ten minutes. Mr Trethowan, I ask you to give me a few days. I ask you . . . as a gentleman.'

Oh God! What a word to choose. She could hardly have hit on a worse appeal, hardly have flung at me a word less likely to ingratiate itself. What had gentlemanliness been, from beginning to end of this affair, but self-seeking and shoddy pretension? But I had no case. I did not know that I ever would have a case. And I wondered what she would have to live for if her family, one by one, was put up in dock, on trial for shabby thefts.

'You have my word,' I said, pulling up. 'As a policeman.'

I stopped by the station entrance, and got out to get her luggage. She summoned a porter by raising a finger, and stood there, rigid, angular, waiting.

'One thing puzzles me,' I said, knowing this was the last time I would see her. 'That evening at Knightley. At the Wrekin. I just can't somehow see you acting the part of a hotel maid.'

She looked at me, as if making a decision, and then suddenly, screwing up her mouth, she let fly in the broadest cockney, in tones of almost cheerful vulgarity: 'Can't yer, then? But yer don't know me at all, do yer? Family charades. Every Christmas. I always did the skivvies.'

And resuming her frozen posture, she walked off into the dark of the station, leaving me to reflect that from the beginning I had totally misjudged her, that really she was a most astonishing woman.

Five days later I heard that she was dead.

CHAPTER 18

Endings

I talked a bit to the Princess about the whole busines
She told me about Bill Tredgold, and how he had bee
interested in her public engagements, and what charitie
she patronized, and who was on their committees. Sh
seemed not at all affected by the fact that this interest ha
led to his death. She was more interested in Lad
Dorothy, but hardly at all worried by the idea she migh
have committed murder. She kept saying over and over
'Golly, think of poor old Dot having a great passion in he
life. You can't imagine it, can you?'

And she giggled. I think the Princess finds the idea c
anyone over thirty having a great passion in their live
frightfully absurd and amusing. I imagine she is going t
sail through life, gaily leaving behind and around her th
wreckage of other people's lives. The rich are differen
from us. They take more for granted. Especially they tak
people for granted. But perhaps when she comes to b
thirty, and then forty, she will find that other people ar
less willing than before to cover up, to pick up the pieces

They put Nuneaton and Stourbridge up on trial, an
the overwhelming evidence ensured they each got fou
years. They are serving it in the best possible conditions
and Nuneaton is actually in an open prison that use
once to be a stately home. The evidence against the olde
men was found to be too frail to stand up in court, so i
effect they got away with it. I didn't worry too muc
about that. Old people in the dock always seem to m
more a sad than a salutary spectacle. I regretted mor
that they never got anything on the repulsive Edwin, s

that he got away scot free. Except that the family shipped him off to Tasmania, a highly traditional thing to do in those circles. I imagine he is bored to sobs, but someone told me the other day that Tasmania is the only state in Australia where gambling is legal, so perhaps the family would have done better to choose New South Wales.

Jan and Daniel were home for the Whitsun break not long ago. We took Daniel to the National Portrait Gallery, to see what Lewis Carroll and Beatrix Potter looked like. With a typical child's perversity he preferred Mr Gladstone, and he was tickled pink by a picture of Charles II, because he said he had sausages in his hair.

But the picture he really liked, and one he stood in front of for ages, was one called 'Queen Victoria Presenting a Bible in the Audience Chamber at Windsor'. It shows the Queen handing over the Good Book to some benighted black, the whole doubtless designed to represent the conquered savage receiving the benefits of British religion. There's the savage, kneeling, looking all handsome and picturesque. There are Vicky and Albert, standing, looking neither. There, gazing benevolently on, are the politicians, Palmerston and Lord John Russell, I would guess. And there, in the background, dark, a mere shape, an outline, is a dim figure that for a long time you do not notice, one that can only be the lady-in-waiting.

Whenever I see that picture in the future, I am going to think of this case.

When we came out of the Gallery, I put Jan and Daniel on a bus home to Maida Vale, and walked down towards St James's Park and New Scotland Yard, where I was to go on evening duty. As I crossed the Mall, a limousine sped by, and I saw the Princess was inside. She waved. I did not know whether she waved at me, as there was a knot of tourists nearby, and it was a typical royal wave. I did not wave back.